NO
VIRGIN

NO VIRGIN

Anne Cassidy

HOT
KEY
BOOKS

First published in Great Britain in 2016 by
HOT KEY BOOKS
80–81 Wimpole St, London W1G 9RE
www.hotkeybooks.com

A CIP catalogue record for this book is available from the British Library.

ISBN: 978-1-4714-0578-5
also available as an ebook

1

This book is typeset using Atomik ePublisher
Printed and bound by Clays Ltd, St Ives Plc

Hot Key Books is an imprint of Bonnier Zaffre Ltd,
a Bonnier Publishing company
www.bonnierpublishing.co.uk

Part One

One

My name is Stacey Woods and I was raped.

My best friend, Patrice, told me to write this story. She's strong and probably the only person I know who can persuade me to do things I don't want to do. She's given me instructions. I'm to start at the beginning and take my time with it. *Don't leave a single thing out*, she said, *however bad it is*.

But it's not always easy to put things in the right order.

After the rape I didn't leave straight away. I was so shocked. I stayed in the bathroom with the door locked. I sat on the floor beside the toilet and felt the cold tiles against my legs, my toes curled on the ceramic floor. I heard my name being called over and over but I didn't respond. *Stacey, you all right? Come on, Stacey. Come out, Stacey. It was only a bit of fun*. After a long time, when it had gone quiet, I turned the lock and opened the door a crack and looked out. He was still there. He smiled at me. I couldn't stay in the bathroom forever, so I walked out and picked up my things from the floor and the bedside cabinet. I kept my eyes down the whole time. I ignored what was going on around me and I got dressed and walked to the door.

He gave me three twenty-pound notes. They'd just come

3

out of a machine and were crisp and sharp and I took them with care in case they cut my skin. I folded them into the palm of my hand and left. I walked to Oxford Street. It was almost six and the pavement was teeming with people. I felt myself carried along by the tide of shoppers and commuters until I edged my way to the road. I put my hand in the air and hailed a taxi. It was something new that I'd learned to do. When the cab stopped I showed the driver the three twenty-pound notes so that he knew I could pay. I gave him my home address.

The cab drove slowly through the rush-hour traffic. I sat in the corner of the seat and let my head rest against the window and watched the city go by. Everywhere people were on their way home from work, walking swiftly, heads down, jackets and cardigans over their arms because of the heat. Men in suits had their ties off or pulled low. The sight of their open collars gave me a churning feeling in my stomach and I held my knees flat together and my whole body tightened and stiffened.

When the cab got to Stratford I asked the driver to pull up at the end of my road. I paid him and walked off down my street. My bag was heavy, the straps digging into my shoulder, so I let it drop down and hugged it to my chest. Two young boys were walking in front of me heading a football to each other, shouting and laughing. They were seeing how long they could go without dropping it. One of them was counting – *twenty-eight, twenty-nine, thirty*. I stepped out onto the road to pass them.

Just as I reached my house the front door opened and my mum came out.

'Where have you been, Stacey? I've been worried about you! Where did you stay? What were you doing?'

4

My mum's hair was wet and there was a towel around her shoulders as if she'd been in the middle of washing it. Jodie must have been watching out of the upstairs window and seen that I was coming. For two nights I'd been away and I hadn't explained where I'd been staying. Mum was upset, tugging at the edges of the towel.

'Stacey, what's been going on?'

I shook my head. I couldn't answer her. My sister, Jodie, was standing in the front porch holding her baby, Tyler, on her hip. She stared at me for a few moments and then turned back into the house. My mum tried to put her arm around me but I didn't want to be touched right then, not by anybody. I gently pulled away. From behind I could hear the young boy counting his headers – *thirty-eight, thirty-nine, forty* . . . I walked into the hallway.

'I can't explain, Mum. I've got to see Patrice,' I said. 'I'll talk to you later.'

I left my mum gaping at me. I dropped my bag on the hall floor and went back out and headed for Patrice's house. I had to speak to her, to tell *her*. I ran all the way. I banged on the door instead of using the bell and her mum answered. She said Patrice wasn't in but I saw her falter and glance back into the hallway when she said it, so I knew she was lying. When she shut the door I stood at the end of her front garden and sent three texts to Patrice one after the other, but the house stayed quiet and closed against me.

I went home. My mum opened the door for me. Her hair was dry now but pulled roughly back off her face, not styled as it usually was.

'Stacey . . .' she started.

5

'I can't talk now,' I said. 'I'm so tired. I just want to lie down.'

She looked hurt, her mouth stretched across her teeth. She stood aside though, so that I could go upstairs. If I couldn't be with Patrice then I wanted to be alone. When I got to my room my bag was there on my bed. I upended it and watched as the stuff I'd been carrying around for the last few days fell out. In the middle of it was the glossy Selfridges bag.

It gave me a start. I'd almost forgotten about it. I held it up and watched the Whistles dress slither out, still wrapped in tissue. I grabbed hold of it and folded it in half and half again until it wouldn't fold any more. Then I shoved it into the bottom of my wardrobe.

It had been bought and paid for, but I didn't want it any more.

In school, the next day, I got in early and found Patrice sitting with Shelly and some other girls. When I tried to catch her eye she looked away. She was hurt because I'd gone away without telling her. She'd sent me loads of texts and I hadn't answered them. She didn't know that I'd *tried* to see her three nights ago after the row with Mum and Jodie.

When I finally cornered her, alone, in the corridor, she stared up at the ceiling like she often does when teachers ask her questions she can't answer, like, *Why didn't you do the homework?* Or, *Why are you late?*

'Look, I'm sorry about the last few days. Please speak to me,' I said.

The cuff on her school shirt was unbuttoned and I wanted to grab hold of it. I often held onto bits of her clothing – the tail of her hoodie or the sleeve of her jumper. She was affectionate

6

towards me too, linking my arm or occasionally giving me a hug as if she hadn't seen me for months. This time I didn't try to touch her because there was something icy about the way she was standing.

'Sorry, do I know you?'

'Come on, Patrice. Don't be like this!'

'Like what?'

'Blanking me. I need to talk to you. There's something I need to tell you . . .'

I felt a pebble lodge itself in my throat.

'Oh, right. So for three days you just disappear. You don't answer any of my calls or texts. You don't respond on Facebook. You just disappear off the face of the earth. Brutal.'

'I deliberately kept my phone off.'

'Not true!' she said, pointing a finger at my face. 'You texted your mum.'

'Just to stop her calling the police out!'

'I was worried. You couldn't have contacted me?'

'I'm sorry. I was trying to get away from *everyone*.'

'Even me?' she said, looking hurt.

How could I explain?

'I was in a state. In any case, there's this thing I need to talk to you about.'

'Well, now *I'm* sorry. Because I don't have time to listen to a part-time friend.'

And with that she flounced off. Shelly appeared at the end of the corridor. When Patrice reached her she took her arm and led her off. I felt the tears coming, so I turned away and headed for the toilets and splashed my face with cold water.

Later I went to the dining hall and got a drink and sat in the corner with my back to the wall. Patrice was across the hall being loud and joking with a bigger group of girls. One of them was standing behind her doing her hair. I was stung with jealousy because I loved doing Patrice's hair. It was long and she often wore it tied up, like a horse's tail. There were endless things that could be done to it: plaiting, beading, twisting, making it into a bun or sometimes just using a comb to keep it sleek and knot-free.

I should have answered one of her texts. Something simple like, *I'm spending some time away. Be in touch*, ☺ *Stacey*. I was angry, though. I had needed to see her that night after the row with my sister but she wasn't available and I'd taken offence and decided to look after myself.

Now I regretted it.

She was my best friend even if I wasn't hers.

Some of the girls with Patrice were looking over at me. Patrice was deliberately looking away. She even turned her shoulder to me so that she wouldn't accidentally see me out of the corner of her eye. I crossed my arms as tightly as I could. I was trying to hold my misery inside. Even as I sat like that I could feel it struggling to get out.

Before leaving school I had to have a meeting with Ms Harper, the head of year, who was asking about my unauthorised absence of two days. It took a number of shrugs and me looking down at the ground for ages for her to realise that I wasn't going to give any details.

'Is it because of things at home? Is that why you stayed off?'

I shook my head, but there was truth in that question.

'How are Jodie and the baby?'

My sister, Jodie, had a baby when she was fourteen. She had to leave school in year nine. It was something I didn't like to talk about.

'They're fine. OK.'

'Is that why you stayed off? To help Jodie look after the baby?'

'No! My mum helps her. She has my mum. She doesn't need me.'

'Because your grades will slip if you take time off school. This is year twelve. A levels are important.'

Mrs Harper made endless notes on a form in front of her.

I walked home alone. The school playground had cleared; there were just a couple of stragglers kicking a football around. I took my jacket off because it was warm; the sun was on my back. As I turned the corner into the high street I saw Patrice standing outside Costa on her own. She was waiting for me, I knew. I felt this little flutter in my chest. I walked up to her.

'Hi!' I said.

'Hi yourself,' she said.

'Hair looks good,' I said.

Patrice shook her head so that her ponytail bobbed.

'Where've you been?' she said, still looking put out.

'I . . .'

'Are you going to tell me or not?'

She stood with her hands on her hips as if she meant business. I wanted to tell her to relax. Of course I was going to tell her about the row with Jodie and then running away and meeting Harry.

But there was something I had to tell her first.

'I was raped,' I said.

Her face dropped. She was speechless. She didn't even say, *Brutal*.

Two

Patrice took me back to her house.

She linked my arm tightly.

She has been my friend since year ten. We sat side by side in our English set and became close within days. In class she is bright as anything, always answers first and sorts out any problems there are with poetry criticism – my worst subject. She isn't that good at getting her assignments in on time though, whereas I'm usually up to date with my work. That's not the only difference between us. She's tall and I'm five foot two. She's loud and I'm quiet, shy almost. She's had five boyfriends and I've just had the one. She's a good dancer and can sing songs after hearing them only once. I veer away from anything public. I like my own space. She's very popular with other kids and likes to spend time with them. I prefer it when it is just us two.

It sometimes causes stress between us.

I love Patrice's house. She is an only child and lives with her mum and dad. It is always quiet there. Her mum is usually in one room reading or doing some work on her laptop. Her dad is mostly at a computer or sitting in front of the television watching football. Patrice's bedroom isn't that tidy but you can tell that any mess is her doing. No one goes into her bedroom without asking her. It is her space. Not like my own house where my mum or my sister seem to breeze in and out of my room whenever they feel like it. Patrice's bedroom has a calm feel. There are private things of hers around, her laptop open, old diaries from years gone by. I know, for a fact, that if I pulled back her top drawer I would find a packet of condoms there, because Patrice is positive that neither her mum nor dad would poke around in her space.

I often stay over at Patrice's house at weekends. It is a relaxing place where she and her parents seem like equals and are always chatting or doing things for each other. When it gets late her parents go off to bed and Patrice and I sit up for as long as we like, watching DVDs or flicking through the channels. Sometimes, if the weather is good, we creep down to the end of her garden and get onto her trampoline, which she's had since she was ten years old. Her mum and dad had wanted to sell it or pass it on to a charity, but Patrice held on to it. It is a huge hexagon shape and has a net around it and we climb onto it and lie on our backs, talking about what we are going to do with our lives. Sometimes we take out tumblers full of freezing-cold white wine and drink them while looking up at the stars. It's peaceful and serene and we both whisper secrets and gossip, our voices disappearing into the darkness.

That day, though, we were sitting in her room. She was on a chair and I was perched on the corner of her bed. I explained what had happened to me. I didn't go into a lot of detail. I was brief and to the point. She was shocked and shook her head.

'You *have* to go to the police,' she said.

'I can't.'

'Why?'

'Because it was my own fault!'

'That's a ridiculous thing to say. Did you *ask* him to rape you?'

'No!'

'Did you tell him to stop? Did you say *no*?'

'Yes!'

'Then how can it be your fault?'

'It's complicated,' I said. 'You had to be there . . . I misunderstood . . .'

How could I explain without making myself look like a complete fool? A girl who couldn't see what was happening because of her own silly daydreams. It was better not to say anything, so I shut up.

Then Patrice sighed loudly, pulled me over to her dressing-table mirror and made me sit down. She picked up a brush and pulled my hair back off my face. She brushed it through for a while, one stroke after another, and I felt my shoulders soften.

'You'll feel better if you get it all off your chest,' she said quietly.

I shook my head. She didn't know the half of it.

She pulled a tail comb from a drawer and parted my hair at both sides and lifted the top tresses. She made some thin plaits, taking her time, gathering them together so that they sat on top of my head. She'd done this style for me before and I'd liked it a lot. She scrutinised it in the mirror from time to time and twisted her mouth up to one side, just the way she does when we're trying to find extended metaphors in a poem.

'You have to find a way to talk about this, Stacey. The police need to know,' she said. 'Have you told your mum? Or Jodie?'

'No.'

As if I would tell *Jodie*. I pictured my sister that very morning walking up and down the landing with Tyler on her hip. She was talking on her mobile phone and Tyler was arching away from her, looking round to me. Jodie ignored him and me and talked loudly as if she was the only person in the house. I pictured myself telling her I'd been raped. There would be initial sympathy, but as I began to unpick the details of what had taken place I imagined my sister's expression being one of amazement, which would quickly turn to derision. Her older, more sensible sister, the one who *hadn't* got pregnant at fourteen, had run away from home and got herself raped. The thought of it made me cringe with shame.

Then I thought of Mum standing beside her, puzzled, confused. *You did what?* she might say, incredulous. In the last few years my mum had shouldered the burden of Jodie's mistakes and problems. *Oh, Stacey, you're so sensible*, she always said to me. *You'll get a good education and a great job. Thank God for one sensible daughter.*

I'd let her down.

14

'I can't tell them. I can't tell anyone. I don't want to talk about it any more.'

'What if this happened to someone else? What if he did it again and you could have prevented it?'

'I don't know. I can't be responsible for what might happen to other people. Don't put that on me. Haven't I got enough to be miserable about?'

I felt tears coming. Patrice handed me a box of tissues.

'Budge up,' she said.

I edged over on the chair. There wasn't much room but she sat down beside me and her arm went round my shoulder. I could see both of us in the mirror, our heads angled towards each other. I was lucky to have a friend like her.

'Right, stop, listen,' she said, playing with some of the strands at the front of my hair. 'If it's so *complicated* then you can write it all down. Every single thing that happened, and I'll read it. There are rape counsellors we could go to. They will read it. Maybe, if you feel up to it, the police could read it.'

'Like a book?' I said, with a half-laugh.

'Don't make it too long and don't have lots of description in it. I hate books with lots of description. Meanwhile, if you see *him*, just ignore him.'

'I'm not likely to see him. He lives in Fulham.'

She stood up, all bossy and businesslike.

'Well, if he contacts you by phone, don't talk to him. You got that?'

I agreed because that's what I do when Patrice tells me to do something. It all sounded simple the way she said it. But she hadn't needed to tell me not to see him or speak to him again. I had no intention of doing that.

I never told her about the text he had sent me that morning.

Really like you. Let's meet up again xxxx

Just reading it had made my stomach twist. That I would keep to myself.

Three

It's hard to know where to begin this story. When I met Harry in Shoreditch? When I left home? Or did it start with the row with my sister?

I got twelve cards for my seventeenth birthday: one from Jodie and my mum; one from my dad and his girlfriend, and the rest from school. The best one was from Patrice. It opened to a pop-up picture and there was the tune of 'Happy birthday to you, happy birthday to you . . .' I also got a card from Benji Ashe, which said *Lots of lurve xxxxx* and which I folded in half and put straight in my bag.

I got money from my mum and dad and some chocolates from Jodie. My best present was from Patrice. She bought me a book on fashion – *Twentieth-Century Style* – which I immediately opened up. It was second-hand and she said she'd got it from eBay. It had page after page of glossy pictures of fashions from the past. Patrice kept apologising that it wasn't new but I didn't mind that at all. At the back, sandwiched between two pages, was a packet for a wedding-dress pattern. It was old fashioned, the paper yellowed, but the actual pattern looked to be still inside. Patrice hadn't known it was there and looked a little embarrassed, but I absolutely loved it, loved the fact that someone had left it there. I put it in my bag to be looked at later but I kept thinking about who had owned it and the person for whom the wedding dress was made. It gave the book an added layer of interest, knowing that a real dressmaker had owned it. Throughout that morning, when I had a chance, I slipped it out of my bag and glanced through the sections, hoping to find something else.

It was a brilliant present, perfect for me.

I had recently decided I wanted to work in the fashion world. I wanted to be a designer. It wasn't something I talked about at home and I didn't make a big deal of it at school. I was aware that saying it out loud made me sound like the dozens of other kids who wanted to be football players or *X Factor* stars or models. The only person who knew was Patrice. In the last year or so, I'd become fascinated with clothes and style. I'd got into sewing and making things. I hand-sewed cushion covers or napkins or scarves. I helped Patrice to take in waistbands and hem up sleeves. I followed sewing blogs and took pictures of things I'd made and sent them in. I collected magazines and old patterns and had scrapbooks of interesting outfits I'd seen. I was always looking on market stalls for old cut-offs of fabric and had a stash in my bedroom so that I could add decorations to garments.

I had a sketchbook in which I designed clothes. There were pages of simple line drawings of dresses, trousers, suits and coats. I wasn't just dreaming. I was planning out my future so that I could get onto the right courses. I'd researched it and I'd bookmarked the London College of Fashion on my laptop.

I hadn't said anything about it to Mum or Jodie. I'd kept my magazines and the stuff I'd downloaded about courses and the fashion industry in my bottom drawer underneath my jeans. It was neatly tucked away in envelope files marked *Careers Assignment*. It was my private business. I wanted to keep it to myself.

When I got home from school that day Mum was already in from work. She was still in her smart clothes and around her neck was the lanyard that held her identity tag. She'd shaken off her shoes though, and was wearing the red slippers with the cat face that Tyler so loved. I sat down beside her and showed her my cards and the book Patrice had bought for me.

'These are lovely, Stacey,' she said.

There was an ashtray on the arm of the sofa.

'Jodie smoking again?'

I could hear my sister coming down the stairs. I looked around the room. The armchair by the fire that she usually sat in was covered in bits and pieces of baby clothes. There was a half-filled bottle of formula by the cushion and on the carpet were three pairs of Jodie's shoes, discarded.

'Doesn't she ever clear up?' I said.

'Don't start, Stacey. She's got a lot to do with the baby.'

That wasn't true. When Mum was home from work she usually looked after Tyler while Jodie did her hair or her nails or read magazines. When Mum was at work it was either me who took him or he got left in his playpen or his pushchair to entertain himself.

The door opened then and Jodie walked in with baby Tyler on her hip.

'Hi, Stacey,' she said, her voice high, a little forced. 'You don't fancy spending some quality time with Tyler, do you?'

Tyler was twisting around to see me. I softened immediately. Tyler was a sweet baby with lots of smiles for everyone. He wasn't at all like his father, a surly fifteen-year-old from the next street who visited him every couple of weeks and stood as far away from him as he could.

'Sure,' I said, picking up my stuff and taking Tyler on my hip. 'He can come up to my room.'

Tyler felt damp and smelled bad.

'Does he need changing?' I said.

Jodie shrugged, picked up the ashtray from the arm of the sofa and sat down in her armchair. Dismayed, I took Tyler upstairs to my room. It wasn't the first time I'd come home from school and found Tyler damp and unchanged.

After I cleaned him up I let him lie on my bed. I took out a soft toy from my bedside cabinet. It was a small brown monkey that I'd made for him, called Charlie. It was furry with stitched-on ears and eyes and a big smile. Tyler held him in one hand and then moved him towards his mouth. He was so predictable. He liked to taste every single thing. I plumped up the pillows around him so that he couldn't roll off the bed. Then I sat down with my back to the headboard. Every few moments I took hold of Charlie and made him do a silly dance in the air, then I gave him back to Tyler.

After a while I got changed out of my school clothes and put on a clean top, some jeans and sandals. I took a look in my schoolbag. I had some homework to do but decided not to unpack my laptop and papers until later, after Tyler had gone to bed for the night.

Oddly, I wasn't relaxed. I looked around my room. The sight of it usually calmed me but today I felt a little uncomfortable and I wasn't sure why. I let my eye rest on various things: the chest of drawers, the wardrobe, the storage unit in which I kept all my sewing things. I looked at the hooks on the wall above it where scarves and bits of fabric hung, my big chair in the window and the small table beside it. Then I looked back to my chest of drawers and realised what was troubling me. The top drawer was slightly open.

I made sure Tyler was OK and I went across and opened the drawer. It was where I kept my toiletries. A couple of bottles had fallen over. The lid of one of them was loose and liquid was seeping out. I righted it and tightened the lid. Someone had been rifling through my things.

Jodie.

My sister couldn't do the one thing I had asked her to do and that was to stay out of my room and my things. Without another thought I swept Tyler up and went downstairs, my feet barely touching the steps. The living room was full of cigarette smoke. Jodie was sitting with her feet up on a stool. Outside it was bright sunshine, but she chose to sit in front of the television. My mum looked round and saw me holding Tyler.

'Jodie,' she said. 'Baby.'

Jodie stubbed out the cigarette.

'Have you been in my room?' I said, placing Tyler down on the sofa next to Mum.

'No.'

Jodie and my mum glanced at each other. That was all it took, that one-second look, and I knew my sister was lying.

'What were you doing in my room?'

'Nothing.'

'But you were in there?'

'Just for a minute. I was looking for some conditioner. I'd run out of mine.'

'Conditioner? Does that mean you've taken mine?'

Jodie shrugged.

'Where is it?'

'In the bathroom.'

I looked at my mum. 'You said you wouldn't let her go into my room! After last time you promised me. You said my room was my own, that it was private.'

'It was just a bit of conditioner, Stacey. She wasn't in there more than two minutes. I stood at the door.'

'She could have waited and asked me!'

'Don't raise your voice, you're upsetting Tyler.'

'Yeah,' Jodie said.

I looked at both of them. Something was twisting up inside my chest. Tyler was still holding Charlie, the monkey, and I was breathing rapidly, afraid to speak in case I said things I'd regret. My sister got pregnant at fourteen: stupid, idiotic, pathetic. She had ruined her life. It was *easy* to get contraception but she hadn't been bothered. She'd let some halfwit boy from the next street get on top of her and give her a baby. Now all she did was to move from her bedroom to the living room while at the same time offloading her baby onto Mum or me or anyone who'd have him. She was fifteen and a half and her life had shrunk down to daytime television. The sight of her disgusted me.

'Don't go in my room,' I said quietly, with force. 'Don't ever go in my room again.'

I was about to turn away and go back upstairs when I heard

22

her laugh. I looked back round. She was sitting forward, both elbows on her knees.

'Fashion designer!' she said.

'What?'

'You're going to go to the London College of Fashion and study design? That's rich, that is. You know you need exams for that. Just because you can sew up a cushion cover doesn't mean you can design clothes for a living. You need to be artistic for that.'

'That's enough, Jodie,' my mum said.

'She's been through my stuff!'

I looked at my mum in fury. She was hopeless.

'I thought you said you were at my room door while she looked for the conditioner? You said she was in there two minutes and yet she's found my careers stuff. You left her. Didn't you? You left her in my room!'

'I honestly don't know why you are getting so upset, Stacey. I think you should calm down.'

'It's my room. MY ROOM!' I shouted.

Tyler started to cry.

'Now look what you've done,' Jodie said.

I walked out and went upstairs. My throat was hot and I was on the edge of tears. I went straight to my chest of drawers. I pulled open the bottom drawer. My jeans had been moved around. I looked underneath and saw that my folder of information on fashion courses had shifted and the flap had been folded back, some of the printouts inside were sticking out at an angle.

I slammed the drawer shut.

I sat on my bed, my fingers woven together, tight with frustration. It wasn't the first time Jodie had been in my room.

How often had I argued with Mum about it? I just wanted some privacy, some space of my own. The previous time Jodie had helped herself to my T-shirt because she hadn't bothered to put her own in the wash. Then, when I found it crumpled up in the corner of the sofa, I'd demanded a lock on my room. I'd even gone to stay at my dad's for a night in a fury. When I got home my mum had promised that she would not let Jodie go there. She had sworn she wouldn't allow it.

But that was Mum. She was hopeless when Jodie started whining and asking for things. Why couldn't she stick up for me? I hadn't got pregnant. I hadn't messed up my life. I was still working hard and looking forward to going to university. I didn't sit in front of the television all day, sneaking a crafty cigarette while my baby was having a nap.

Mum and Jodie; they had always been so close. Jodie, as a little girl, had spent most of her time on Mum's knee or leaning into the crook of her arm. If Mum put her down she would scream the place down. *She's just a little anxious*, Mum would say, shrugging her shoulders. Jodie was no longer the baby of the family but she was always there, at Mum's side, whispering to her, asking her favours. If only she took as much notice of Tyler.

My throat was fiery and I was on the brink of crying, so I stood up, picked up my bag and my phone and my charger. Patrice would let me stay the night at her place. I could go straight to school in the morning. I wouldn't have to see Jodie or Mum again until I'd calmed down. I packed some smart clothes for school the next day and made sure I had everything I needed for an overnight stay.

I was still angry when I went downstairs, so I left the house without saying goodbye.

Four

I headed for Patrice's, walking quickly, puffed up with indignation. I was picturing Jodie poking about in my drawer. I remembered her laughing and saying, *Fashion designer!* as if I shouldn't have an ambition.

Just because she had given up on life, she wanted me to do the same.

We hadn't always been at each other's throats. When she was younger I took care of her, especially when Mum and Dad were out at work. I got her dressed and played with her, read stories to her; we watched television together and I took her round to her friend's house and picked her up later. She loved coming into my room and looking through my school things. *Can I tidy up your felt tips?* she'd say and then spend ages slotting them into their plastic holder, making sure the colours moved along the continuum from yellow to black. Even after the divorce we were close. In her early days at secondary school I used to pass by her form room to make sure she was all right. She was always introducing me to her friends. *Meet my big sister*, she'd say, even though some of them were already taller than me. At first she would wait around for me after school and we'd walk home together, but somewhere along the line it changed. She had new friends who she hung around with, surly girls who wore thick mascara and talked behind their hands. She started to ignore me in school and walked around the house in total silence. If I spoke to her she said, *What?* in an irritable way. She got into trouble with teachers and kept telling Mum to leave her alone.

She became a stranger.

Then I began to see her with the boy from the next street, Philip Day. They were usually lounging around in the park or sitting in a bus shelter or in the kitchen eating from McDonald's wrappers. While she was pregnant Philip Day disappeared for a while. After Tyler was born Jodie began to look ten years older, her shoulders rounded, her mouth constantly pursed up to one side, a cigarette in her fingers.

My phone rang. I took it out of my bag and saw *Mum* on the screen.

I didn't want to answer the call. I turned it to silent and put it in the pocket of my bag. I slowed down, wanting to shake off my temper before I got to Patrice's. I turned onto the high road and walked for a while. Then I saw Shelly Goodman, from school. She was coming out of a corner shop and was talking on her phone. She had her head angled towards her shoulder and was ambling rather than walking, as if she had no particular place she had to be. She stopped by a bench and perched on the back of it, as if she was waiting for someone. She ended her phone call and looked around.

Shelly was one of the popular girls in our form class. As soon as she was dropped off at school in the morning, and almost before she had closed the passenger door, other girls would rush over and start talking rapidly to her. In the common room she was always talking to Patrice about work they were doing in their Law A level, Patrice raising her voice with excitement. Patrice wanted to be a barrister. It was her burning ambition to defend people who had been accused of crimes they hadn't committed. She was always reading out examples of miscarriages of justice, her finger floating above her iPad to keep her place.

I knew Shelly and Patrice often sat together in their Law lessons and I knew that they helped each other out with notes and handouts. Walking towards room SS28 with Patrice I usually felt tangled up inside. She would go in to Law and I would walk on to AR3 for Art. As I left her at the door I could hear Shelly's voice singing out, *Here, Patrice,* no doubt having saved a seat for her.

I often asked Patrice about her. *What were her plans? Did she want to be a barrister? Did she have a boyfriend? Did she like music? Where did she live?* Sometimes Patrice would answer, but often I felt her getting a bit irritated. Just last week she said, *Honestly, Stacey, ask her yourself. She sits across the room from you in form group!* But I only really spoke to Shelly in passing. The fact that she and Patrice shared an A level meant that they had a friendship that I was excluded from.

When I saw Shelly in the street close to Patrice's house I was confused. She lived in Forest Gate, a bus ride away. I wondered why she was there. I should have walked up to her and tapped her on the shoulder and said hi. I found myself stopping though, turning my back on her and looking into

27

the window of a dusty hardware shop, sidestepping the rows of plastic boxes and buckets that sat outside.

That day, being my birthday, I'd asked Patrice if she'd like to go for a pizza with me. It would be my treat and then we could go back to her house and watch a DVD or listen to music. She'd said she couldn't. She'd said that her mum was going to put some henna into her hair and so she was staying in. She said we could do it on Friday, which was a better day anyway because it was the end of the week.

I hadn't minded.

Turning my head slightly I could see Shelly out of the corner of my eye. She answered her phone again and talked for a few minutes, then she walked off. I watched her go, hoping that she would head towards a bus stop or in the direction of the Tube. When I looked further I saw Patrice standing up the road, on the corner of her street. Shelly was walking towards her.

It was a shock.

I quickly went inside the hardware shop and looked out through the window. I could hear the man in the shop saying, *Can I help you, miss?* I ignored him and watched Shelly and Patrice standing in the street, talking, smiling. Then Shelly threaded her hand through Patrice's arm and they started walking.

I felt my neck tighten and I swallowed a couple of times. I could hear the shop owner's voice again, so I walked outside. Shelly and Patrice were no longer there. They'd turned back into Patrice's street.

I was filled with anguish. Why didn't Patrice just say, *I can't come for a pizza tonight because I've said I'd meet Shelly?* Why not just be honest? Deep down, though, I knew the reason; she was keeping it from me because she knew I'd be upset about it. Her and Shelly's friendship was growing, and Patrice knew I wouldn't like it.

I stood there for a long time, watching the end of Patrice's road. I imagined them walking along, talking about law and the things they were studying. Maybe Shelly wanted to be a solicitor or a barrister. It would be a sensible ambition, one that Patrice would share. Maybe that's what they were talking about: courses to choose, which university to go to. Possibly they would both apply to the same one and live in a shared house.

Possibly, later on, when it was dark, they would both go and lie on the trampoline and look up at the sky. Maybe they would get round to talking about me. I thought that after all their chat about dreams and ambitions Patrice would tell Shelly that I wanted to be a dress designer. I pictured Shelly, her head flat on the rubber surface, saying, *She wants to be in fashion? Huh! No chance of that!*

I knew I couldn't go to Patrice's house that night.

Five

After seeing Patrice with Shelly I headed for my dad's place in Shoreditch.

He was away on holiday but he'd given me a key a year or so before and I'd threaded it onto my keying so I always had it on me. I got the Tube and walked through the early-evening crowds towards his apartment block. The streets felt sticky beneath my feet and people bustled past me looking thirsty and fed up. I turned off the main road and had to step off the narrow pavements to let people go past.

I used the entry code to let myself into the building. I went up in the lift and along a winding corridor until I got to his door. On the ground was a dark pink West Ham welcome mat with the faded word *Hammers* on it. I let myself in. The place was silent and stuffy, so I walked into the living room and unlocked and opened the windows. Cooler air came in but there was a whiff of the street about it; exhaust fumes and spicy cooking smells. The vertical blinds wafted in the breeze. There was iron trelliswork that made a gate across the window, giving the impression of a balcony. My dad had told me they called it a 'Juliet balcony' after *Romeo and Juliet*.

31

It was a calm place to be, but not as calm as Patrice's house. I so wished I was there with her instead of here on my own.

It was my dad's first proper home since he and my mum had split up four years before. Even though he was a paramedic and drove an ambulance, he'd had to live in shared houses with only a bedroom that was private. My mum had kept the family house, but it meant that she'd had to go back to work full-time in the local council planning office.

I could hear noises from outside the apartment: music from the floor below, traffic from the street, voices calling out and, in the distance, an alarm ringing. I sat on the floor with my back against the sofa. Finally I could relax. The apartment was still and calm. There was no chance of Jodie appearing or Tyler breaking into sobs, or the constant drone of television programmes.

It was sparsely furnished. There was a long sofa and a massive television opposite. Built up around the set were box sets of police dramas that my dad loved to watch over and over. The other end of the room was the kitchen area and in between his pushbike was fixed to a frame that he'd screwed into the wall. His bedroom was next door, and across from that was a tiny bathroom. When he'd first moved in he'd said there was only room to swing *a tiny cat*, which had made me shiver, picturing a kitten being swung round.

He wasn't due back for a couple of days and I knew he wouldn't mind me sleeping there. He'd always said I could visit any time. He knew how I felt about Jodie and the baby and he'd told me to use his flat to get breathing space. *You're always welcome*, he'd said, so I'd gone there a lot up until the last few months when he'd got together with a woman called Gemma.

Lately I hadn't felt quite so relaxed there.

Gemma was with him in Corfu. He'd met her through his job. She was involved in a car crash and his had been one of the ambulances sent out to the accident. Then he'd bumped into her later in Sainsbury's. They'd started talking and one thing had led to another. She was pleasant to me but I always felt that I was in the way. Before Gemma there had been plenty of room for me and Dad to stretch out on the sofa. After she came it was the two of them sitting side by side and me up the other end or on the floor. She brought her own box sets too. Programmes that were soppy, the kind of stuff my dad would not have watched but now he did. And I was sure she kept glancing at her watch when I was round, as if counting the minutes until I went.

I made some food and helped myself to a cold beer. Shutting the fridge, I saw that it was dense with papers and leaflets held to the door by a variety of magnets. A fixture list of West Ham football matches for the season that had just finished was partly covered by two take-away menus from local restaurants that Dad liked. There were postcards that had been sent from different parts of the world; on the top was one from Niagara Falls and another from the Sydney Opera House that had the word *Amazing!* written across it in felt-tip pen. There was also a giant crossword, which had been overlapped by other stuff. Some of the clues were filled in but most of it was blank.

My mum and dad did crosswords when they were still together. After dinner some nights they would sit across the dining table while Jodie and I (for a while) packed the dishwasher and tidied up the kitchen. I could hear them from where I was, my dad reading out clues and my mum trying to guess the answer; *seven across, six letters, 'Lawn game', first letter 'c'* . . . Sometimes she got annoyed: *I can't make this out, why don't you use a pen!* And I remembered the finished crosswords being faint and almost unreadable. My dad always used a highly sharpened pencil in case he put in a wrong answer. When it was completed they'd do a high five, something that made me and Jodie roll our eyes – a brief moment of camaraderie for us.

Then one day they stopped doing crosswords. Dad would get up from the table first, saying he had things to do. Or Mum would get up and clear the plates and tell us that she would load the dishwasher and I would stand at the top of the stairs and hear the deepening silence from below.

I missed my dad. While Jodie sidled up to Mum I had always been Daddy's girl. *How's tricks, kid?* he would say when he got in from work. *Are you looking after those two?* And when Jodie was getting round Mum he would roll his eyes at me. Sometimes he slipped me extra pocket money, saying, *Don't tell Jodie!* During the last four years it had been me visiting him at the shared houses and him and me going to the cinema or for a walk along the South Bank. Jodie always preferred to stay with Mum.

I drank the cold beer and watched television for a while and pulled my mobile phone out of my bag. There were two texts from Mum and one from Patrice.

I opened Mum's texts one after the other.

Don't be angry. Just come home. Please xxxx

I'm sorry about your room. Please let me know where you are. You know how I worry xxxx

I knew if I didn't reply she would get more and more upset. She might even go to Patrice's or come over to Dad's apartment to try to find me.

I answered her messages.

> **I need a bit of space. I'm staying at a friend's (not Patrice). Will go to school tomorrow. See you in the afternoon.**

Then I opened Patrice's text.

> **Are you having a nice time on your birthday? LOL ☺☺**

It had been sent twenty minutes before.

I wondered if Shelly was sitting beside her. Were they talking about me? Was she feeling guilty? I considered sending one back asking her about her hair and whether the henna had taken evenly. I didn't though. I just tucked my phone into the side pocket of my bag and let out a dramatic sigh.

I was alone and feeling sorry for myself.

I watched television and had two more of my dad's cold beers. Then I went into his bedroom and took the spare duvet, sheet and pillow from his cupboard and made up the sofa to sleep on. Before I turned off the light I made a list. It was something I often did when I was fed up. I divided the page in half and wrote *Good* on one side and *Bad* on the other. I wrote down some of the Good things in my life.

- The London College of Fashion
- Tyler
- Good grades
- Finally finished with Benji
- £371 in savings
- Patrice

I made a list of Bad things in my life.

- Jodie
- Patrice

I was aware that Patrice was in both lists. I looked at my phone again and wondered whether to answer her text. I decided against it. After a long time tossing and turning on my dad's hard sofa, I went to sleep.

In the morning I felt better. I showered and put on my smart clothes for school. I put away the bedclothes and made sure the apartment was tidy. I wrote a note for my dad to say that I'd stayed there and that I owed him some beers. Then I locked up. I intended to go to a cafe, have some breakfast, then head on to school. Once there I would pretend that I hadn't seen Shelly meeting up with Patrice.

Everything would stay as it was. When school was finished I'd go home and make peace with my mum and Jodie and spend some time with Tyler.

But it didn't happen like that, because an hour or so later I met Harry.

Six

Shoreditch was full of cafes. It was early, just after seven thirty, so I took my time choosing which one to go to. I turned off the main road and headed for an old-fashioned place that had a blackboard outside. It was called Katie's Kitchen and I liked the look of it. I sat at a table in the corner, by the window. I'd awoken positive and sunny but now, as I sipped my tea and broke off bits of my muffin, the idea of going to school and acting as if nothing had happened seemed mad.

I pictured myself walking into the common room and seeing Patrice sitting in the middle of a group of girls as she usually was. Shelly might be there and they might glance at each other just for a second – the way my mum and Jodie had the previous afternoon – and I would know that they were keeping their meeting a secret from me. I would be like a deceived boyfriend and I would go along with it, a party to my own deception.

Why not ask Patrice about it? Why not say, *Did I see you meeting up with Shelly last night?* What if she said, *Yes?* She might use a defiant tone, as if to say, *What's it to you? I can be friends with whoever I like.*

I might lose Patrice's friendship. That was something I could not bear.

I finished my muffin and tea. It was coming up to eight o'clock. If I was going to go to school I should make a move. I sat there though, and eventually got up, went to the counter and bought myself a yoghurt. When I sat down again I got my sketchpad out of my bag and began to draw. I sometimes did this if I had time to kill. I loved looking at how people dressed. I watched them walk by, on their way to work, one hand holding a takeaway coffee, the other holding bags or newspapers. I sketched their outfits, one after the other, flicking the page until the next person came along.

After years of school uniform, including the 'smart' clothes I had to wear in sixth form, I was fed up with conformity. Outside school everyone wore the same things: jeans, leggings, sports clothes; even the girlie stuff you could buy was dictated by half a dozen shops. It was only possible to find 'unique' clothes if you went to a vintage shop or market stall, and they had been made for differently shaped women. So I was always looking for girls, women or guys who stood out from the crowd, who had done something different with their wardrobe.

My face was turned to the window and I was concentrating so I didn't hear someone pull out the chair beside me and sit down. When I'd finished drawing a girl in patterned leggings with a short kilt and a silky shirt I sat back, wishing I had some colours with me just to note down the combinations and the shades of the garments that I'd seen.

'You an artist?' a voice said.

A young man was sitting at the end of the table. I looked at him.

'Sorry?'

'With the sketching, I mean. Are you making sketches for a painting?'

He had a cup and saucer in front of him and beside it a tiny cafetière. There was a croissant on a plate. On the opposite seat he had placed a holdall.

'No, I just draw the clothes that people wear. I'm interested in clothes.'

He smiled. He had dark curly hair cut short, but longer on the top. He was good-looking, his skin tanned as if he'd just returned from a foreign holiday. His teeth were even and white.

'Fashion? London is a good place for that. Some people say it's the fashion capital of the world.'

'I thought that was Paris,' I said, closing my book, slipping it back into my bag, afraid that he might see some of my simple sketches.

He put his hand out across the table.

'I'm Harry.'

It seemed too formal. I let his hand sit in mid-air, feeling embarrassed. He held it there though, determined to make me shake. His face broke into a smile and I put my hand out and brushed his fingers.

'I'm Stacey,' I said, shrugging, ill at ease.

'Are you on your way to school?' he said.

'I might be . . .'

'Sorry. I'm just nosey.'

He took a bite from the end of his croissant, holding it over the plate. Flakes of it floated down. I picked up my yoghurt and began to eat it. He was wearing dark trousers and an open-neck shirt. Around his neck was a lanyard with an identity tag hanging from it. While eating I glanced up from time to time and made out the print: *Montagu International College.* He saw me looking at it.

'It's my school. It's in Kensington.'

I nodded. It sounded posh, like a private school.

'I . . . I go to school in Stratford.'

I didn't know if he'd heard me.

'*Stratford*, where the Olympics were?' I said.

'I *know* Stratford. *Stratford-atte-Bowe*. It's in *The Canterbury Tales*.'

I smiled at this.

'*The Canterbury Tales* is this long poem by—' he said.

'Chaucer. I *know* who wrote *The Canterbury Tales*.'

'Touché.'

He poured the coffee from the cafetière. Then he pulled his mobile out of his shirt pocket and read something on it. I realised that I was staring at him and he was a complete stranger. I imagined him telling his mates at school, *This weird girl from the East End was ogling me while I had my breakfast. It was embarrassing.*

'I have to go,' I said.

He put his phone down beside his cup and saucer.

'I bet you're in year ten,' he said.

'No!'

'What, eleven?'

'I'm lower sixth. Almost finished the first year of my A levels!'

'You look too young.'

'Well, I'm seventeen. Actually I was seventeen yesterday.'

'Happy birthday for yesterday. If I'd known you yesterday I'd have bought you a card.'

'What year are you in?'

'Ah! Lower sixth, same as you. Supposed to be doing A levels. That's if I don't get expelled first. I've got an appointment with my head of house at nine, and if I don't attend, that could be it for me!'

'Expelled?'

'Last chance. I've done some bad stuff. If I don't toe the line, they'll show me the door.'

'What did you do?'

He put one elbow on the table and looked like he was thinking about his answer.

'I'll tell you what I did if you show me one of your sketches.'

I frowned.

'What's wrong with your sketches?'

'Just amateur. Personal stuff. Only for me to see.'

'Likewise. My bad deeds are only for me to know.'

'Maybe I'm not that interested.'

'OK. I understand.'

I huffed. What was I doing in deep conversation with this complete stranger?

'Just one sketch,' he said.

I pulled my book out of my bag. I flipped back a page and showed him one that I'd done a week or so before. I hadn't been in a rush so it wasn't too rough.

'Not bad,' he said. 'You know, if you're interested in fashion I know someone who works as a buyer in Selfridges. They have all sorts of fashion collections there. I'm sure she'd have a chat with you. Have a look at your designs.'

I ignored his attempt to prolong the conversation about my drawings.

'Your turn. Why are you in trouble?' I said.

He was about to take a sip of coffee but stopped. He was smiling but I could see that he was working out what he was going to say.

'I stole a car and drove it to Oxford to see a girl.'

'Oh.'

I'd been expecting something less dramatic, like smoking in the toilets or swearing at a teacher.

'I thought I was in love with this girl and I was sitting in the school library doing prep and I just had to see her.'

His voice was suddenly serious and he was looking down at the table, rubbing his thumbnail against the wood.

'I *had* to go then and there. So I took the master's keys and his car and went to Oxford.'

'You took a *teacher's* car?!'

'Yep,' he said, grinning.

'How come you weren't expelled right there and then?'

'It's my dad's old school, his dad, his granddad. The whole male side of the family went there. Besides, my dad helped pay for the new library. They're not really going to expel me.'

I shook my head with wonder. This was another world.

'But I have to pretend to be trying, which is why I've got to go.'

'You've got to get to Kensington by nine?'

'Yes,' he said, putting his phone in his pocket. 'Got a taxi coming. Come outside and wait with me.'

'I was going myself . . . I have to be in school . . .'

'Keep me company.'

I put my stuff away and stood up.

'Gosh, you're tiny!' he said.

He was tall and broad. He had his holdall in one hand and he used the other one to open the door for me and I went outside.

'Are you sure you're in the sixth form?'

'I am.'

A black taxi had turned off the high street. It had its indicator on. I stepped back and got ready to wave a goodbye but he grabbed hold of my wrist and put something in my hand. It was a card. The name *Harry Connaught* was printed on it with an email address and a mobile number.

'You're really sweet, you know. And pretty. Call me, if you want to meet the buyer who works in Selfridges. Or call me if you just fancy another chat in a cafe. In fact . . .'

He plucked the card back off me and produced a pen from his pocket and wrote on it.

'Just *call* me . . .'

He gave it back as the taxi pulled up. I looked down at it. He hadn't *written* anything at all. He'd drawn a heart on it. My face broke into a smile and he gave me a little wave as he got into the back of the taxi. I saw him lean forward and say something to the driver. Then it drove away and he was gone and I was standing a little dazed on the pavement. I looked at the card again. I couldn't help remembering the story he'd told. *I thought I was in love with this girl . . . I had to see her . . .*

I felt strange. I felt like I'd just been at the centre of some sparkling lights and now they had dimmed.

I made myself walk on towards the bus stop, but when I reached it I carried on going. In my hand I held Harry's card and felt its sharp edges digging into my skin. In the midst of my bad mood about Jodie and Mum and Patrice and Shelly, there was this warmth radiating through me. This boy had taken me out of myself.

I thought I was in love with this girl . . .

He wanted me to call him.

I couldn't go to school. Not with all this to think about.

Seven

I went to Oxford Street. I got off the Tube and walked towards Selfridges. It was gone nine and I should have been in Art. I knew that Patrice would wonder where I was, but I also knew that she'd be in Law with Shelly sitting next to her. I'd already sent a text to school to say that I was unwell.

I thought about not being at home that morning when Tyler had woken up. It was usually me who picked him up out of his cot while Jodie was sleeping. I was happy to change him and pop him into bed with me for a few minutes before I had breakfast. Then I would hand him over to Mum, who looked after him until she had to go to work. Then Jodie usually dragged herself out of bed to take over.

I had no guilty feelings about it. I was walking along as though I hadn't a care in the world. Up ahead was Selfridges. It was a big slab of a building that filled a whole block and looked palatial. I headed for the main entrance, which was in the centre and had metal doors and columns at each side. I pushed against a heavy door and strode in as if I was a regular and had been going there all my life. In fact, I'd only been a couple of times before, mostly shopping in the sales with Dad.

It wasn't my kind of store, a bit too posh for me. But now that *Harry* had mentioned it I wanted to go there.

Harry Connaught.

Just saying his name in my head made me smile. As if he was a prize that I had won. I walked through the make-up and perfumes department and caught a glimpse of myself in a mirror. I was *grinning*.

I made myself adopt a serious expression and browsed the ground floor of the shop. The marble floors and mirrored counters were a bit like the shops in the Westfield shopping centre near where I lived, but Selfridges had a sort of grandeur to it. It felt old, as if generations of people had shopped there; women in long dresses and bonnets and men in top hats. I passed the leather goods and saw the designer names: Prada, Dior, Chanel. On some of the counters were giant white ceramic vases filled with red silk roses. The place exuded classiness.

I hadn't noticed any of these things when I came shopping with my dad.

Women's fashions were on the upper floors but I didn't want to rush up there yet. I wanted to sit somewhere on my own and think, to pore over the meeting with Harry in the cafe.

I went into the food hall and sat at a high counter and ordered a tea. It was expensive. The receipt was fancy and I noticed at the bottom it gave a Wi-Fi code. I got my laptop out and turned it on. It took a while because it was old and had been repaired a couple of times, but eventually it booted up. I went onto Google and tapped in *fashion buyer*.

I drank my tea. There was strong smell of cheese from the food hall. I wrinkled up my nose, not liking it.

I looked at my screen. I read over a couple of pages of information but I already knew what a fashion buyer did. They had to be skilled enough to identify the trends from the fashions shows and work out what the public would like and wear and how much they would be prepared to pay for it. A shop like Selfridges would have more than one and they would have to know about every facet of the fashion industry. It was an important job. It wasn't what *I* wanted to do, but it would be mad if I could meet one and talk to them about their day-to-day work.

Harry knew someone who worked as a buyer in Selfridges.

I checked my emails. There was a message from Dad. I opened it.

Hi, Stacey! Coming home tomorrow and looking forward to seeing you. Gemma and I have a lovely prezzie for you. See you soon. xxxx

I felt my lips pucker up at the mention of *Gemma and I*. I shut down my laptop, firmly locking my feelings of irritation away. I thought back a couple of hours to when I was in the cafe in Shoreditch and Harry sat down beside me. He must have watched me sketching for a few moments before I noticed him there. What had he seen? A small girl with jaw-length hair, wearing a smart white blouse and dark skirt. Her lips would have been pursed tightly together as she concentrated on drawing passers-by in their outfits.

What did he think? Was he *attracted* to me?

I looked around, embarrassed, as if someone else might be reading my thoughts.

Things like that didn't happen to me.

47

By *things* I mean *boys* didn't happen to me. Patrice had no problem with boys, she seemed to draw them to her, but I got tongue-tied and awkward and in any case never really enjoyed their company that much. The boys in my school seemed to be constantly on display so that everything they said was directed towards some invisible audience. Rob or Jonesy in Art seemed to say stuff like, *That's three grade As so far this term!* and flick their eyes around the class to see if anyone else was listening. Or Jerry, who walked home in the same direction as me, repeated my questions, as if there were loads more people who should be hearing them: *Where am I going this weekend? What's my favourite band?* And they hardly ever looked straight at me but past my shoulder, as if trying to see if there was anyone else around who was more interesting.

Harry just *talked* to me. He seemed interested in me, keen to see my sketches. He told me something very personal. *I thought I was in love with this girl . . . I had to see her . . .* No boy, not even Benji, had said anything that personal to me before.

I felt myself smiling again, a feeling of jitteriness in my chest.

I packed up my laptop and went off up the escalator to the second floor where women's fashions were. I walked through, looking from designer to designer – some names I had never heard before: Miu Miu, Peter Pilotto, Balenciaga, Marc Jacobs. Some of the labels had small seating areas in between the displayed clothes – zany sofas and bright, puffed-up chairs. There were floor-to-ceiling mirrors everywhere. The clothes were displayed on brass rails, sometimes only one or two items hanging there. This gave the impression that these clothes were rare, that not many of them had been made. Unlike the shops that I went to, which had hundreds of the same dresses, tops, jeans and jackets. I didn't bother to look at the prices. These kinds of clothes were completely out of my league, and even if I had the money to buy them (I thought of the £371 pounds I had in the Nationwide), I wouldn't have a clue where or how to wear them.

I got my sketchpad out and continued browsing. I came to the Whistles range, a name that was familiar to me. There was a chair nearby so I sat in it. My eye was taken by a dress at the back of a rail. It was striking and simple at the same time. It looked like it was made from chiffon, white with a black design on it. It was a sleeveless dress, empire line, and flared out in thin pleats from underneath the breasts. There was a black panel in the front. It was lovely. I drew on my pad, adding labels to describe the style. I sat back and wished I could have designed it.

I loved designing unusual dresses, even though I never wore them and didn't own any. There was something about them that was so romantic. They seemed to imply special occasions: weddings, parties, ceremonies. Dresses weren't to be worn for slouching around the house. They were for going out, meeting people. They didn't fit my life or the lives of my friends (Patrice had a couple of pretty dresses in her wardrobe, but she hardly ever wore them). Dresses seemed to belong to a past time when women wore gloves and hats and stoles. When I designed dresses I always imagined them worn by tall women who had secretive smiles and could click their fingers for a waiter. I never saw myself in them.

But this Whistles dress was something that might not look out of place on me.

I began to copy some of the other designs. After sitting there for a while a man in a light grey suit appeared. He was standing stiffly, his legs together as if he was on guard duty.

'Excuse me, madam, may I ask what you're doing?'

'Oh . . .' I said, flustered, closing my pad. 'I . . . I'm working on a fashion project for college. I'm just looking at your collections. I hope that's OK.'

'Are you from the London College of Fashion?'

'Er . . . Yes. Yes, I am.'

I held out my sketchbook. He glanced down at it politely.

'That's good. Well, our staff are always happy to help any budding designers! Who knows? Some clothes of yours could be here one day.'

He walked away and I felt mildly exhilarated. He had accepted my story of being a student at the London College of Fashion. I didn't look odd or out of place. I got up and began to walk towards the escalator. I'd spent long enough in the store. As I headed for the main doors I realised it was almost eleven o'clock. I couldn't go back to school because I'd rung in sick, and anyway I didn't want to.

Then I had an idea that made me feel excited. I got my phone out and the card Harry had given me. I found an alcove to stand in, leaning back against the wall. I could feel my heart banging against my chest and I tried to ignore it. Every bit of common sense was telling me not to make a fool of myself.

And yet I entered Harry's number into my phone and composed a text.

Hi, Harry. We met this morning in the café in Shoreditch. I'm up in Oxford Street now. Any chance of you introducing me to that fashion buyer you said you knew? I can make it any time. Stacey

I read it over two or three times. I paused and looked around, as if someone might be watching, knowing that I was about to do something foolhardy. I searched each word for hidden meaning. There was no hint of attraction or sense that I was trying to get to see *him*. It was a businesslike text.

How would it read, though, when it reached him? Would he smile knowingly, as if he'd been expecting it? Or would he be surprised?

At least I wasn't making the first move.

He had done that by giving me his card.

I pressed *Send*.

Eight

I couldn't hang around Selfridges forever so I went through the heavy glass doors and walked towards Oxford Circus. I was heading for the London College of Fashion. I knew the address and I'd looked at a map to see where it was. I wasn't going to go in but I wanted to look at the building, and I was curious about the kind of students who went there.

Before I left Selfridges I turned the sound off on my phone and tucked it down into the bottom of my bag. My mood had clouded over a little. All my bravado, browsing through the fashion ranges, sketching clothes, dwelling on the meeting with Harry, had been pushed aside by the text message I'd sent. The thrill of doing it, of pressing *Send*, had been followed by the instant worry of whether or not I would get a reply. Up to that point I would have remembered a rather nice experience when a posh boy talked to me and admired my sketches. Now, though, I'd taken it one step further, and if he didn't reply then the morning's events would leave a bad taste.

So I placed the phone somewhere I couldn't see it.

I tried to look in shop windows as I passed them but my feet were carrying me quickly towards the London College of

53

Fashion. It was in a street behind Oxford Circus and I made my way there, feeling excitement building up. I'd already spent a while on their website looking through the requirements needed to be accepted as a student. Once I'd found the relevant section I said it over and over to myself, and now I knew it off by heart. *Students interested in fashion design would ideally need to have studied subjects such as art, design, textiles or photography for A levels/BTEC level 3 and should have a portfolio of design work.* I loosely fulfilled this requirement and I'd shown it to my art teacher, Miss Previn, so that she could guide me in the right direction.

It was a modern white building that was above a row of shops on Oxford Street. The sign over the entrance said *University of the Arts London*. I paced up and down for a few moments, then built up the courage to go in. I walked up to a display and picked up a brochure, giving a polite smile to a security man. I slid it into my bag and went back outside. I stood across the road, out of the way of people walking by, and watched. All sorts of people went in: young, old, male and female. They were black and white and Asian. Some people were smartly dressed; others were scruffy. One or two wore bizarre outfits. Nearly all of them had lanyards around their necks holding identity cards. I wondered if I would fit in there. I looked down at myself in my smart sixth-form clothes. How would they view me if they saw me then at that very moment?

I got my phone out. It was almost an hour since I'd left Selfridges and I looked at the screen with trepidation. The message icon had the number two next to it. I opened it quickly but was immediately disappointed to see that I had one message from Mum and one from Patrice. My mum's was brief.

Message from school to say you're absent. Where are you? I'm worried about you. Please ring xxxxxx

I had forgotten that the school would send a text to Mum. I felt bad. My anger at Mum for letting Jodie go into my room had abated and I knew that she would be upset. At that moment she was probably at work trying to concentrate but looking from time to time at her phone in case I had called her.

Patrice's message was light and friendly.

Are you OK? ☺ ☺

I put the phone in my pocket. I didn't feel up to replying to either of them. The one person I wanted to hear from hadn't contacted me. I started to walk away from the college entrance and found myself in Cavendish Square. It was a busy thoroughfare with cars and lorries queuing around it. In the middle was a small green area though, and there were people walking through it with dogs, mums pushing buggies, some tourists pausing to look at maps. Most of the benches were used by people eating. I realised that it was lunchtime. I wasn't hungry though, so I sat down heavily on a low wall by the perimeter.

Harry wasn't going to reply to my text.

He probably had tons of girls who liked him. I was mad to think he might have been interested in me. He was much more likely to go for someone like Patrice. She was attractive and had lots of confidence, whereas I was small and shy and nothing out of the ordinary to look at.

Benji Ashe had been my only boyfriend. He was a friend of Greg's, a kid that Patrice had been with for a while. He was in the upper sixth, so he wasn't in any of my classes. Patrice and I had been sitting in McDonald's one afternoon when Greg came in with Benji. We got talking and then started seeing each other.

He wasn't very tall, so my short height suited him. He was quiet and didn't say much, but that first day he grabbed my hand as the four of us walked away from McDonald's and when we got to my street he gave me a hard, wet kiss before going off with Greg.

I thought you might like him, Patrice had said.

At first we spent time as a foursome and it didn't really matter that we had nothing in common. After those few times with Patrice and Greg I saw him on his own and we went to the cinema and for a walk and there was an uneasy silence the whole time. I tried to talk but he was tongue-tied. The only thing he seemed to be interested in were the vinyl records he collected. Then he talked non-stop, telling me how he searched the internet for rare tracks and how he bought and sold discs via the web. He played them to me and I enjoyed some of them, but he insisted on making me listen to particular bits and listed the instruments and the singers, all dead a long time before.

Being with him was boring until the kissing started. Then he was very eager, trying to get his fingers inside my top and making me breathless with long kisses. He was confident and pushy. I liked it. He always backed off when I stopped him and he didn't seem unhappy about it. He sent me lots of messages, signing them *With Lurve*, which made me smile at first.

After a while I wondered why I bothered. Most of the time we spent together was taken up with sexual stuff: kissing, petting, going further and further. It wasn't unpleasant. Whenever we stopped we would both laugh at the state we were in, our clothes ruffled and our buttons and zips undone. Trouble was, after the giggling Benji went silent and I was fed up trying to make conversation.

One night we didn't stop. I had condoms in my bag that Patrice had made me buy so it seemed the obvious thing to do. Patrice had had sex with two different guys to my knowledge, so had some of the other girls we hung around with.

Why was I waiting?

It was over in minutes, maybe seconds. Then there was the embarrassing bit of getting dressed – finding my pants and jeans in the muddle of his bedclothes, putting them on awkwardly by the side of the bed, not being able to look him in the eye. I'd wanted to say, *Is that it? Is that what all the fuss is about?* I wanted to be able to laugh about it, but he had turned away and seemed to be unlacing and relacing his trainers. Then he showed me a new disc he had acquired. A rare 1960s Tamla Motown LP. He played me a couple of tracks but then I said I had to go.

I knew as I walked away from his house that night that I didn't want to see him again. I told him in the sixth-form common room the next lunchtime. He shrugged it off but I heard from Patrice that he was upset.

That was my only experience with a boy.

Until now.

I pulled my phone out of my bag. I was impatient. I wanted *something* to happen. My phone seemed like some kind of link to Harry, my previous message stretching out between us. I stared at the screen, willing his name to appear.

As if by magic, it did. **Harry**. I gasped and opened the text.

**Love to see you, little Stacey. How about
outside Marble Arch Station at 2.30?**

I sat up straight, my back and shoulders puffed up with delight. I sent a reply.

Great! See you then ☺

I spent a few moments deciding on the smiley, but then I thought, *Why not?*

Nine

I waited across the road from Marble Arch Station for Harry. I'd spent the last hour and a half in a sandwich bar. I'd had something to eat and read a newspaper that someone had left behind. I'd sent my mum a text telling her that I was OK and would be in touch later. I'd thought about sending a text to Patrice but decided not to.

I was so nervous about seeing Harry that I was grinding my teeth.

I caught a reflection of myself in a shop window. I was wearing my sixth-form uniform (no jeans, no trainers, no skin showing, not too much jewellery and absolutely no tattoos). Over my shoulder was my bag. It was big enough to hold my school stuff, laptop and the spare clothes I had with me since I left my house the previous day. The bag had patchwork pockets on it, into which I usually put my travel pass, my phone and my purse. On one of them I'd sewn a variety of tiny buttons that I'd bought in a charity shop for ten pence. It was a small thing but it made my bag one of a kind.

All in all, though, I looked like a schoolgirl. A *young* schoolgirl. No matter what I wore or how much make-up

I put on, I always looked younger than my years. My height was the problem. If I could grow a bit it would add years onto my life.

'Hi!'

Startled, I turned round and Harry was standing there with another young man. He had walked up without me noticing. He looked different. He had changed his clothes and was wearing shorts and a T-shirt. He looked more like the boys from where I lived.

'Stacey, this is my mate Dom. He wanted to come along and I said I was sure you wouldn't mind. You don't, do you?'

Dom was smaller than Harry, with longer hair tucked behind his ears. He had on bleached jeans, flip-flops and a T-shirt. There were strings of tiny beads around his neck. He looked like he'd just walked off a beach somewhere.

'No.'

I felt a twinge of disappointment. I'd expected Harry to be alone. I'd *hoped* it would just be him and me. I gave a big hearty smile to cover my feelings.

'Hi!'

Dom held out his hand. I put my hand out and he grabbed it firmly and shook it. I decided that shaking hands must be something they taught at the Montagu International College, because no one from my school did it.

'You both got out of school?'

'Exam practice. Free study.'

Dom and Harry smirked at each other.

'Right, I've made a plan,' Harry said, and he took my arm, leading me off along the pavement, managing to weave in between other shoppers. 'We go to see Mary Potter at Selfridges. She's the buyer I told you about. She used to be my brother's girlfriend. She's really nice. The two of you can have a talk and meanwhile Dom and I will go for a drink in this pub I know. Then afterwards you can join us. How does that sound?'

'Good.'

We went across the road and headed for Selfridges.

As we entered the store I began to think about what a bizarre day this was turning out to be. Yesterday, on my birthday, I went to school and then home. Just a mundane day that ended in a row. Today I was in another world. I was in central London instead of in school in Stratford, and I was with a boy I had only just met. I pictured Patrice's face when I eventually told her all about it. *Brutal!* she might say, looking suitably impressed.

'I'll be in the men's while you take Stacey up,' Dom said.

He peeled off from us as we went up in the escalator. I gave him a tiny wave as he disappeared from sight.

'He's nice,' I said.

'He's a good mate.'

I was on the step above Harry on the escalator and my face was level with his.

'What did your head of house say?'

'The usual. Be a good boy, knuckle down, make your father proud.'

He was staring at me, his eyes very direct. There was a sudden tension, a shift in mood. I wanted to look away but his gaze seemed to hold me there. And I felt his hand on my waist, pulling me towards him.

Then he kissed me.

It was hard and brief, his lips twisting slightly to the side.

I was surprised and embarrassed, but inside there was a flicker of heat in the pit of my stomach. When we came to the top of the escalator I got off. I was unsteady and didn't quite know where to go. He put his arm round my shoulder and lowered his mouth to my ear.

'I've been wanting to do that since I first met you,' he said.

'When you first saw my sketches,' I said, trying to make light of it.

'Maybe,' he laughed.

As we walked on his arm dropped down because we were passing other shoppers. We stopped at some doors. There were seats adjacent to them and Harry sat in one of them and gestured for me to do the same.

'We wait here,' he said.

He got out his phone and began to tap in a text.

The seats were close together and his arm was brushing against mine. He felt warm and I saw that his forearm was covered in fine hairs. I had an urge to stroke his skin with my fingers and I thought about the kiss minutes before.

'Did you go home? To change your clothes?'

'No, did it in school. Left my bag there, in my locker.'

Just then some swing doors opened further along and a woman came out.

'Harry!' she called out loudly. 'How good to see you.'

Harry got up and walked towards her and gave her a hug and a kiss on each cheek.

'Is this your friend?' she said, walking towards me.

'Stacey, this is Mary,' Harry said.

She had long brown hair and was wearing dark trousers and a light, floaty top. She had a pair of glasses perched on her head, holding her hair back. She put her hand out for me to shake (again). Her nails were long and dark maroon. She smelled of perfume and peppermint. I guessed she was in her late twenties.

'How nice to meet you, Stacey,' she said.

She was tall.

'Thank you for seeing me . . .'

I seemed to shrink further down, as if I was a child among grown-ups. She turned to Harry and began chatting, asking him about his brother and his parents. Harry was relaxed with her but she was self-conscious – I could tell by the way she was holding the hem of her top, bunching it up and letting it go.

'So, you'll give Stacey the A–Z?' Harry said, after the small talk had finished.

'I will.'

'Text me when you've finished,' Harry said, and walked off before I could answer.

'Come on, Stacey. Let's go upstairs to the offices.'

I followed her out of the shop floor and we went up some stairs. The plushness of the store had gone and the stairwell was grey and chilly. We went up two flights and she talked all the time.

'Did Harry tell you I used to go out with Marty? His brother? Just for a few months. Well, two months and one week. I finished with him because he wasn't the faithful sort. I liked him but . . . So you want to be a fashion designer? That's a good ambition but it's not the glamorous world some people think it is. It's hard work. It's not all fashion shows and designer collections!'

'I know. I just like the idea of creating more individual styles. So people can feel comfortable wearing . . .'

Mary was a few steps ahead of me and wasn't listening. I was irked. I had a realistic view of how hard it was going to be. I'd compared courses. I'd read blogs and personal experiences of people who worked in the fashion industry. I wasn't some child who liked making dresses for their dolls. I was a hard-working and determined student.

At the top of the flight of stairs she stopped and caught her breath.

'I should be fitter than I am. I gave up smoking in January. Well, I did it because Marty didn't like cigarette smoke. He was very particular. My friend Rose said, *You're better off without him*, and she's right, I know, but . . .'

She walked towards some swing doors. She keyed a number into the keypad and the door buzzed open.

'I don't know why I'm saying all this to you, Stacey. Harry's ten times nicer than Marty. You should hold on to him.'

I followed her in, my mouth half open to say something, but she talked on without me needing to take any part in the conversation. We walked through an open-plan office where a number of men and women were sitting in front of computers. She took me into a small room at the corner of the building. The office was tiny but had windows on two walls so was light and sunny. She pointed to a chair and I sat down.

'Have you met Marty?' she said.

'No,' I said, wondering whether to tell her that I had only met Harry that morning.

'Well, I expect you will. So! You want to be a fashion designer. Right, let's see what I can tell you about working in fashion . . .'

Thirty minutes later I left her office. She walked me down the stairs and left me in the same seats where Harry and I had been sitting earlier. In my bag was some stuff she'd printed off from the company website and lists of courses and colleges that were well thought of. She also gave me a book list and some fliers for exhibitions that were worth seeing. She'd been helpful, but amid it all she'd talked on about Harry and Marty and the fact that they had a house in Fulham and a place in the Cotswolds as well as a holiday home in Florida.

Mary Potter had said that she was over Marty, but she clearly wasn't. I'd watched as she'd fiddled with the hem of her silky top and said that she'd never really understood why he'd gone out with her in the first place. Her parents owned a shop and his were bankers. *I think he was slumming,* she'd said a little sadly.

I patted the side of my bag, which had belled out with the stuff she had given me. I hadn't liked her much at first but then I felt sorry for her. She had a great job in an exciting industry and all she could do was talk to a complete stranger about someone she had loved and lost.

I sent Harry a text.

I've finished with Mary. She was really nice and helpful. Thank you.

Seconds later I got a reply.

**Dom and I are in King John pub in
New Bond Street. I'll buy you a drink xx**

I stood up, hoisted my bag over my shoulder and went off to
find the pub.

Ten

I was anxious about going into the pub. Because I look so young I usually avoid them. Patrice and I don't go very often. There have been parties where everyone had to meet up in a pub first. I usually put loads of make-up on and my highest heels and try to look older. I end up looking agitated and guilty though. Bar staff often ask me my age, and even though I lie convincingly it's embarrassing.

So I avoid pubs.

The King John was a couple of hundred metres down New Bond Street on a corner. When I walked up to it I was pleased to see that it was packed. There were people standing outside on the street, drinking, smoking and chatting. I walked in and wove my way through the drinkers and saw Harry and Dom in the corner. They were sitting on two seats either side of a table and there was a spare chair between them so Harry got up and I slid in and looked around, feeling relieved that I hadn't been noticed.

'What do you want to drink?' Harry said.

'A beer, please.'

He went off to the bar. There was a window behind me and I could hear the murmur of conversation from people outside.

I could also smell a faint whiff of cigarette smoke. My bag was on my lap and I didn't know what to do with it. I edged it down the side of the chair. It was a relief to have it off my shoulder. Now that it was full of the stuff that Mary Potter had given me it was ridiculously heavy. Dom was watching me. His eyes took in my bag and I suddenly felt self-conscious about it. The buttons that I'd sewn onto the pocket now looked a little amateurish.

'How did you meet Harry?' he asked.

'Accident. He sat next to me in a cafe. We got talking.'

'Harry's a good talker.'

'Yes. He's friendly. That's not always the case with boys. At least the boys I know.'

'We're all very friendly round here.'

'Where do you live?'

'Chelsea.'

'You go to Harry's school?'

'I do. You?'

'I go to Stratford East Academy. It's near where the Olympics were held.'

'Stratford-atte-Bowe?'

'In Chaucer's time maybe. Now it's just plain Stratford.'

He nodded approvingly. He was tucking his hair behind his ears and looking a little smug and I felt a bit irked. I wondered if these private-school boys thought that no one else had ever been taught *The Canterbury Tales*. I gazed around the bar and remembered when Harry had mentioned it this morning. Then it had seemed funny and sweet, but now I was feeling mildly insulted by it. Was I being too sensitive? Or was it just that I had been immediately attracted to Harry so I hadn't minded him poking fun at me? I could see Harry turn away from the bar. There was barely room to move and he was edging back towards us with three bottles of beer, two in one hand and one in the other. When he reached the table he handed one to me and one to Dom.

'How was Mary?' he said, after drinking a mouthful.

'She was great. Full of advice and information.'

'Did she go on about my brother?'

'She did mention him.'

'Like a hundred times?'

'Well, a couple . . .'

Harry and Dom laughed. I frowned. I didn't feel good mocking her when she'd tried to be helpful. Harry immediately put his hand up.

'You're right. We shouldn't be unkind to poor Mary. But that was your first time meeting her. I've had her going on at me about Marty hundreds of times.'

'How come you see her? I mean, if she's not your brother's girlfriend any more.'

'Friend of friends of friends. We move in the same circles.'

'Right.'

My phone beeped. I leaned down and searched in my bag for it, moving about the papers and leaflets that Mary Potter had given me. I pulled it out and saw that there was a message from Jodie. I frowned and read it over.

**I wish you would come home. Tyler is not well.
Mum can't get off work and I might take him to
A&E because he's got a temperature.**

69

I must have had a dark expression on my face because Harry stopped talking to Dom and looked at me.

'Everything all right?'

'Sure.'

I drank some of my beer. I was choked up. It wasn't the first time Jodie had used Tyler's health to manipulate me. I shoved the phone back into my bag and tried to smile and shrug at the same time. Harry turned back to Dom.

'Did you see that Timothy Bell is doing a gap year in South America?'

'No.'

'He's going to Belize to build a school . . . I quite fancy doing something like that after A levels.'

They began talking about gap years and I felt myself drifting away from them, thinking about the text I had just got. I was angry, seething. I sat very still, sipping my beer, holding it up to my face so that my expression couldn't be seen.

Lately, whenever there was a row or bad feeling between my sister and me she would eventually announce that Tyler was unwell. It was usually after a period of standoffishness – me ignoring her or not speaking directly to her. After a few days of this she would announce that Tyler had an upset stomach or an earache or a fever or all three. I instantly caved in and looked after him. Often he was just a bit cross or overtired or bored. I played with him, gave him a bath, fussed over him and he was usually all right. Jodie was always grateful, saying, *Oh thanks, Stacey. You're so good with him* . . . And even though I was still curt with her, it meant that the row and its aftermath were over.

70

I knew she did it on purpose.

The last time had been a month or so before, when I'd been going to Patrice's birthday celebration meal with her and some members of her family. A Chinese restaurant had been booked and it was a dress-up affair. I was the only one of Patrice's friends who had been asked. I was excited about it for days and Jodie was fed up and grumpy, saying that she *never went out anywhere* and that Chinese food was her *favourite*. I ignored her and on the night of the meal I took a while to get dressed and ready. I wore some dark trousers and a top that I had bought and trimmed with sequins. I was just about ready to go when Jodie burst into my room holding Tyler, who looked red-faced.

'He's not well. He's burning up!' she said.

She held him out to me.

'I can't take him, Jodie. I'm going out. Ask Mum.'

Tyler, who looked tired, started to cry and rub his fist against his face. His T-shirt top was covered in stains and there was something sticky in the front of his hair.

'He's ill,' Jodie said, her shoulders bristling. 'Doesn't that count for more than going out?'

'He's got a temperature. Give him some Calpol.'

It was an uncaring thing to say but I was angry. I knew what she was doing. She was trying to keep me at home. Because she had no life of her own she didn't want me to go out enjoying myself.

'What if it's not just a temperature? What if it's meningitis?'

I wasn't going to fall for it, so I walked past her, picked up my bag and went out. I was too early for the meal, too early to go and call for Patrice, so I walked round the streets, annoyed

71

and upset. I went all the way to the high street and looked in shop windows. When it was time I headed for Patrice's. After a glass of champagne each (except for her dad who was driving) we all went to the Chinese restaurant. When we got out of the car we could see the long table through the window. Every one of the chairs had a balloon attached to it with the words *Happy Birthday* printed on. The atmosphere was festive and everyone was laughing and making jokes.

It couldn't have been more different to my own family.

My phone was in my bag on silent. I managed to not look at it for over an hour while the starters came. Eventually, I went to the toilet and took it out. There were three missed calls from my mum. With a heavy heart I rang her.

'We're in A&E. Tyler's been vomiting and his temperature's high. You should come, Stacey. We need you.'

I ended the call. I saw myself in the mirror. My hair was nice and my make-up was good but my mouth was twisted up with frustration. I went back out to the table and told them I had to go. Patrice's dad jumped up and said he would drive me to the hospital but I refused. I got my coat and left, Patrice waving at me through the window. My chair was empty and it seemed as though the balloon that was attached to it was drooping more than the others.

When I got to the hospital I met my mum and Jodie coming out of the swing doors. Tyler had been checked over and was fine.

'It's better to be safe than sorry, isn't it, Stacey?' my mum said.

We headed for the car park. I held Tyler in my arms and kissed his warm head and his sticky hair. Jodie had pulled out a cigarette and was sucking from it while we walked along in silence in a shivery breeze.

It was a memory that still made me angry. I looked at Dom and Harry and realised that they had stopped talking.

'You're miles away,' Harry said.

He clicked his fingers in front of my face, as if I was in hypnosis. I tried to smile but there was a lump in my throat

'Sorry,' I said.

'We must be the most boring guys on the planet,' Dom said. 'I'm going anyway.'

'Sure?' Harry said. 'You don't have to go.'

'I'm seeing Suzie after college. I said I'd meet her.'

Dom straightened his jeans and tidied up the beads around his neck.

'Bye, Stacey.'

He left the pub and Harry moved into the seat Dom had been sitting in. He was closer to me.

'You all right?' he said. 'Did you get a bad text?'

'No, I've just got a lot on my mind.'

My voice cracked. Was I going to cry? I took a gulp of beer and tried to smile, but my throat had filled up and my eyes had blurred over.

'What's up?'

'I just . . .'

It was hard to explain without it sounding pathetic. *I don't like my sister. She uses her baby to emotionally blackmail me. My best friend likes this other girl more than me.* It was just a list of stuff that showed how weak and inadequate I was. So I told a mad lie.

'I've run away from home.'

Harry looked surprised.

'I had a big row yesterday and I left. I spent last night in my dad's flat because he's on holiday. When I met you this morning I was deciding what to do. I just don't want to go back home. I hate it there.'

As I said it I realised it was the truth.

I did not want to go back home. Ever.

Eleven

A man wearing a creased linen suit asked if he could have our spare chair. He took it away to a nearby table and wedged it in between other drinkers. There was a loud discussion going on and a lot of noise. Over by the bar a group of women were toasting each other, holding their glasses up high and saying, *For Bethany!* On the bar were two ice buckets in which there were bottles of champagne leaning at angles. Bethany was wearing a smart suit and high heels but on her head was a bride's tiara.

I was sitting with my hands together and my fingers woven tightly on my lap. Harry had moved his chair as close to mine as it would go. Then he spoke into my ear so that I could hear him.

'I had no idea that you'd run away,' he said, raising his voice a little. 'Won't your family contact the police?'

I shook my head. 'I told Mum I was going to stay at a friend's until I've decided what I'm going to do. I'm seventeen now. The police won't come looking for me because I'm not in danger.'

The lie was getting bigger. I *was* in touch with my mum so she didn't think I'd run away, but that didn't sound so dramatic.

And Harry seemed so concerned, so caring. I felt that I was the centre of his attention.

'What about your dad?'

'He doesn't get back from holiday until late tonight. He knows I'm unhappy at my mum's. When he contacts me I'll tell him I don't want to live there any more.'

'Can you live with him?'

'No. His place is tiny and he has a girlfriend.'

I pictured Gemma smiling at me, her eyes flicking down to her watch to see how long it was until I went home.

'What will you do? You must be really unhappy.'

'I am.'

I started to tell him about my home life. I told him about Jodie and the baby. His face had an odd look on it – part shock, part awe. A fourteen-year-old girl getting pregnant probably didn't happen in his world. I imagined his family was much more *proper*. Mum and Dad still living together, loads of money, posh schools, houses in the country and in Florida. My family must have looked alien to him.

The one thing I didn't tell him about was my friendship with Patrice and the way I was feeling about it. That was too private.

'I need a break from home. I can't face seeing them again for a while.'

Once I'd said it, it became true. I did need a break from them. A few days or maybe longer. I was seventeen. I was still at school but did I actually have to *live* with them? I imagined going to live at Patrice's. I got on well with her parents and there was tons of room there. Why couldn't I do that? Just until my A levels were done. Then I could go to university and live in halls. Then I remembered Shelly going round to Patrice's the night before and the fantasy instantly fell apart.

Harry emptied his bottle.

'Another?' he said.

'No.'

I'd had two bottles of beer and was feeling lightheaded.

'I ran away once,' he said, leaning forward, fiddling with the hem of his shorts. 'When I was fifteen. It was a Friday night and I'd had a row with my dad. I don't even remember what it was about, but my dad likes to shout a lot and he pointed his finger right at my forehead and I swear I was on the brink of hitting him, but you don't hit your dad. You can't, it's not right . . . So I walked out. I jumped in a taxi. I didn't know where I was going. In the end I got dropped off at Covent Garden. I had a mate from school who lived round there. We spent that night getting drunk and smoking dope. I was sicker than I'd ever been in my life and I rang my brother, Marty. He came to get me and cleaned me up and I stayed with him for a couple of days, and then he took me home and my dad and I had this long conversation where my brother was like an umpire and we made an agreement.'

He spoke with passion. He seemed affected by the memory, as if the emotions were still with him.

'My brother always sorts things out for me. He's the best.'

'*Parents* . . .' I said. 'Aren't they supposed to be the grown-ups?'

'You're right. You're smart, you are, little Stacey.'

I remembered what he'd said that morning. *I thought I was in love with this girl.* Then his voice had had a heaviness to it. I wanted to know about the girl; what she looked like, what sort of a person she was, why he *loved* her. I'd only known him for eight hours and I was jealous of this girl.

'Tell me about the time you took your teacher's car.'

'Oh, that!'

'You wanted to see a girl in Oxford . . .'

'It's embarrassing.'

'Who was she?'

'Melanie. She was a half-cousin of mine. She was nineteen and she drove a black jeep and she broke my heart. She had this red hair, right down her back. She'd never had it cut, since she was a baby.'

'Cousin?'

'Once, twice removed. I don't know. She was at a family Christmas do and we had a lot to drink and I was just bowled over by her. I thought she felt the same. Trouble was she liked someone else better than me. First love. Make a fool of yourself. It happens to all of us. It's all gone now.'

First love. I had never been in love.

'When did it happen?'

'Three months ago. The school contacted Marty and he got a train to Oxford to pick up me and the car. He drove it back to the school and sorted things out with the masters. Since then I've been on a kind of probation.'

'It sounds like it hurt a lot.'

'It did, but it doesn't now.'

I took his hand and squeezed it. He gave a half-smile. I thought he probably *was* still hurting. Being rich and having houses all over the place can't stop you getting a broken heart. I felt emotional, as if we were both joined together by unhappy events. Wasn't that why he had made an impact on me? *I thought I was in love*, he'd said. A lovestruck boy with a runaway girl. It seemed like a story from a movie.

'I've got this great idea,' he said. 'My brother looks after this apartment for a mate of his, a guy from his stockbroker's who's in Singapore for a year. You could stay there for a couple of nights.'

'Oh, no . . .'

'Why not though? My brother uses it himself sometimes. If he goes out drinking and he wants somewhere central to crash, he sleeps there. His friend told him to do that. Marty even lets me and Dom stay over if we want. So there's no reason why you couldn't do it for a couple of nights while you get your head clear.'

'I don't know.'

I'd thought I was going home after being with Harry. I hadn't wanted to, but I knew that all the running-away stuff was a fiction. And then there was the text about Tyler and the fact that he wasn't well (true or not?). In my heart I was running away, but in my head I knew I had to go back.

'If you're nervous, I could stay there with you. I can tell my dad I'm staying with Marty. I'll keep you company.'

'Well . . .'

'I don't mean . . . I'm not saying I would stay *with* you. I'm saying I could sleep in the apartment as well. There are two bedrooms. I just thought you might feel odd in a strange place.'

'I didn't think you meant anything like . . .'

'I didn't. I'm not that sort of . . .'

'I know. I didn't think you were!'

79

'We should both just stop apologising.'

He made a *huh!* sound but stared at me, holding my attention. There was something else in his eyes, pinning me there, making me sit perfectly still. He stroked the back of my hand with one finger and a slow-motion tingle crept over my skin.

'You could text your mum. Tell her you're thinking things over. Then really do that. Stay at the apartment and cool off. You might miss them and decide to go home.'

'Are you sure your brother – or his friend – won't mind?'

'Positive. We're finished here so let's get a cab to my brother's work, pick up the key, then we can have something to eat. Maybe Dom will come round. He could bring Suzie. We could chill out. Have a laugh. What do you say?'

'I'll send a text.'

'I'll just use the toilet,' he said.

He walked away and I tapped out a text to my sister.

How is Tyler?

Moments later I got an answer.

OK.

Brief and to the point. Jodie didn't waste her words. I tapped out a message to my mum.

I'm staying another night with my friend (not Patrice). I'll text you tomorrow.

The pub seemed fuller than before. The hen party at the bar were *all* wearing tiaras and Bethany had added a veil to hers, which hung stiffly round her face. The glasses were being refilled and one of the champagne bottles was standing upside down on the bar.

I could see Harry coming back from the toilet. One of the girls called out to him, laughing, holding out a glass as if offering him a drink. He smiled but skirted round them, making a *no thanks* gesture, and walked back to me. I stood up and he put his arm around my shoulder and pulled me tightly towards him. He kissed my forehead and ruffled my hair, then we manoeuvred our way through the drinkers.

It was mad. To stay out with a boy I hardly knew in the apartment of a stranger.

But I was willing – no, I was *eager* – to do it.

Twelve

Harry hailed a taxi. It pulled up a few metres ahead of us and we walked quickly towards it. He leaned in the window holding a twenty-pound note in his hand.

'Stukeley Street in Holborn, please,' he said.

He seemed so grown up. His accent was crisp like a government spokesperson and he spoke confidently, as though he was used to giving instructions. His tone was polite though, and he opened the car door for me to get in first and had a little chat with the driver about the traffic. I felt like a child again, tongue-tied, awkward. I sat on the seat, putting my bag down in the far corner, taking up as little space as I could. I pulled my seat belt on as the taxi edged away from the kerb and did a U-turn in the road. A car beeped angrily but our driver seemed unperturbed and the taxi drove away smoothly. Harry looked comfortable, his legs apart, his hand holding a handle that was up by the door. In his other hand he had his phone. He'd obviously put his money away. I wondered if he had held it out to prove that he could pay the fare.

It was the first time I had ever been in a black London taxi. My life was buses and Tubes or walking. I'd occasionally called a minicab for Jodie and the baby to go somewhere, and Patrice and I had used one a couple of times when we'd been out late. But I'd never stood on a pavement with my arm in the air trying to attract the attention of a London taxi driver. I'd have been too embarrassed, too awkward. I'd have apologised as soon as it stopped and not been able to say where I wanted to go.

Harry used taxis all the time, it seemed.

I watched Oxford Street go by and felt myself relaxing. It had been a strange day. As if I'd opened the door of Katie's Kitchen that morning and stepped into an alternate universe; me, Stacey Woods, a girl from Stratford, East London (atte-Bowe), in a taxi heading for an apartment off Oxford Street. During the day I'd been in the offices of Selfridges talking about the fashion industry. Just before that, rising on an escalator, I'd been kissed by a prince.

I felt Harry's fingers tapping on my hand in a playful way.

What had happened? Had my miseries of the night before (my birthday) been righted in some way? I didn't believe in God but was there some sort of karma working for me? As if I deserved a better life than the one I had?

I felt Harry's arm slip round my shoulder. I looked at him. He closed his eyes and leaned towards me. His mouth covered mine for an instant and I felt his fingers flicker across my breast. Then he pulled back and sat in his seat as if nothing had happened. It made my chest ache. I glanced in the rear-view mirror in case the driver had been watching, but he was looking straight ahead.

My phone beeped. I took it out and looked at the screen. The name *Patrice* was there. She had left a voicemail for me. I listened to it as the taxi slowed down in heavy traffic.

Hi, Stacey. What's up with you? Missed you at school. Give me a call.

Her voice was light and friendly and I wondered whether to ring her. Maybe when I was on my own sometime I would quickly call her and *say, You won't believe what sort of a day I'm having. I've met this amazing guy* . . .

'Anything important?' Harry said.

'No,' I said.

I gripped my phone though, suddenly missing Patrice. There was no one in the world I wanted to share this experience with more than her. But I knew I wouldn't. The image of her and Shelly walking down her street was still in my head.

When we got to Stukeley Street Harry took his seat belt off and leaned forward to talk to the driver. 'I'm just picking something up here. Then we want to go on somewhere else. Is that OK with you? I'll pay waiting time of course.'

The driver mumbled something and it sounded as if it was all right.

Harry turned to me. 'Marty's coming down to the door to give me the key card. I'll just get it and then we'll go straight back. You OK in here for a minute?'

'Sure.'

I watched him get out and walk off towards a building further along. Just as he got there a man stepped out of a door recess. I guessed it was his brother, Marty. He had no jacket and the sleeves of his shirt were folded back. He was smoking a cigarette and his face broke into a smile when he saw Harry. He was shorter than Harry but stocky, his stomach sticking out like a beer gut. He and Harry talked for a few minutes and then Harry turned round and pointed at the cab. Marty looked across in a cursory way but turned back to Harry and started to speak to him at length. Harry seemed put out. He was looking at the ground as if he was being told off. Then Harry spoke earnestly. He was gesticulating with his hands and pointing to the taxi.

I couldn't read Marty's expression. Perhaps he wasn't happy about giving over the key for me to use the apartment. Most likely his friend was happy for *him* to use it, but a total stranger was another matter. Did it mean I would have to go home after all?

Marty took something out of his shirt pocket and handed it to Harry. Still, though, he was talking and his face was serious. Harry was saying the odd word but nothing at length. Then Harry was nodding as if agreeing to something. Marty put his hand in his trouser pocket and pulled out his wallet. He seemed to be giving Harry some notes.

Marty turned towards the taxi and stared at me. I didn't know whether to wave or look at my phone and pretend I hadn't been watching them. He smiled though, so I raised my hand in acknowledgement.

Harry walked back to the taxi and got in. His friendly face had gone and he looked pinched and angry.

'Hi,' I said. 'Is everything OK?'

He leaned across to the driver.

'Poole Street, off Oxford Street, please,' he said.

He sat back, taking a sigh, his fingers tapping on the seat.

'What's up?'

'Marty says my mum is going to make me retake the lower sixth.'

'How do you mean?'

'I've got to do the whole year again.'

He was exhaling, looking out of the window.

'What? Go back and start sixth form again?'

'Yeah. I missed a bit of time and some of my work hasn't been up to date but . . .'

'Oh.'

'I'll be with younger kids. It's a total embarrassment. It's ridiculous. I could catch up. I promised her I *would* catch up over the summer.'

'Maybe she'll change her mind.'

He shook his head. His mouth was tightly shut.

'She might just be saying it to shock you. Then, in a couple of days, she may give you another chance . . .'

He looked up.

'She's probably trying to give you a kick up the backside. Tell you the worst that can happen, the thing she knows you don't want to do. Then, when you've got used to it, she could relent, set conditions for you to do more work. It might just be strategy on her part.'

'Do you think so?'

'You can talk to your brother, can't you? He could mediate for you. He did it before.'

'Maybe he could. You're right, she might be just saying it to scare me into doing work.'

'So over the next few days you get all your work up to date. And then show it to her.'

'I could.'

'You could go home now and get started. You don't have to look after me. I can get a Tube . . .'

'Oh no. She thinks I'm staying with Marty anyway. No, we're going back up to Oxford Street. We have to get some food and then go to the apartment.'

'What about your work?'

'I'll do some when I get home. She'll *see* me doing it then.'

'Are you sure?'

'Stacey. More than anything, at this moment, I want to spend some time with you.'

I looked away, a blush heating up my face. My hand was flat on the seat and I felt his fingers touching mine. It sent a feeling of yearning through me, a surge that ran in waves across my skin. Something intense was happening and I was spilling over with emotion. I kept my face to the window in case he realised the effect he was having on me.

The taxi seemed to increase its speed, veering around buses, heading back to Oxford Street.

I was really running away from home: from Jodie, from Mum, from Dad (and Gemma) and even from Patrice.

Thirteen

Harry punched a number into an entry pad at the apartment building. We were going into 132 Poole Place, Marylebone Lane, off Oxford Street. He was holding a bag that held four pizzas, which we'd bought from Marks & Spencer. I had also bought a packet of vest tops and some pants. I was looking forward to having a shower and changing out of my school clothes.

The doors slid open and we walked into a small lobby, which had two lifts at the far end. There was no one about. On one side the wall was fitted with floor-to-ceiling post boxes. The other side was covered in polished tiles.

I followed him to the lifts. One came quickly and he pressed number eight. When the doors closed he leaned down and gave me a brief, rough kiss. My hands were full with my bags, but if they hadn't been I would have put my arms around him. Twice before he had kissed me on the mouth. Each time I had been the recipient, as if he was giving me a gift. The first time I'd been too surprised to do anything, but the next time I had wanted to respond, to take his elbows and pull him close. I hadn't had the confidence though.

The lift seemed to stop abruptly and we stepped into a hallway that had the same glowing wall tiles and a dark floor. There were no windows but discreet angled lighting. It was silent and there was a vague aroma of wood. It was very different to my dad's apartment block, where I could always smell something cooking. Harry went ahead and stopped at a solid wood door that had a tiny circle of glass in it. He pushed the key card into a slot and then entered a number into a small electronic pad at the side.

The door opened and we walked in.

The apartment was vast. We stepped into a large sitting room that stretched out towards a wall of windows. I walked towards them, dropping my bags by a long dark sofa. The apartment overlooked the side street we had walked along, but because we were high up we could also see the roofs of the surrounding buildings. Down at ground level I could see lines of cars but I couldn't hear a thing. The windows were shut but the apartment didn't seem stuffy.

'Here,' Harry said.

He stepped in front of me and fiddled with a catch and I could see then that the window was a door. He gave it a push and it opened, letting in the heat from outside. Through the door was a balcony with pot plants and enough room for three or four people to sit. I thought of my dad's Juliet balcony that wasn't a balcony at all.

'Come on, let's have a look around.'

I followed him and he took me from room to room, as if he was on a television property programme and he was trying to sell it to me. There were two bedrooms, both with double beds. There was an en-suite shower room attached to one of them. There was another bathroom down the hall. The kitchen was small but glowing with stainless steel and granite work surfaces, which Harry pointed out. There didn't seem to be a fridge or washing machine, but Harry showed me that they were all there, hidden behind cupboard doors.

'It's amazing. It's all so neat and tidy.'

'There's a cleaner who comes in once a week. Marty organises it.'

The place was sumptuous. I suddenly imagined Patrice standing there beside me, looking around and saying, *Wow!*

'You can have the main bedroom and I'll have the other one.'

'Is it OK if I take a shower and get changed?' I said.

'Sure. I'll put the pizzas in the oven. I'll get some beers out, unless you prefer wine. Marty always makes sure there are drinks here. Dom and Suzie are coming about nine.'

'Beer's fine,' I said.

I went into the bedroom and looked around. A little thrill went through me. How had I got here? With this boy? A chance meeting in a cafe had led to this. It was as if I'd stepped off a tiny rowing boat onto a yacht.

I upended my bag so that everything fell out onto the bed. I put my laptop to one side and sorted through the rest of my stuff. I pulled out the jeans I had been wearing last night and my toiletries. My new tops and underwear were in the Marks & Spencer bag. I picked out my charger and connected it to my phone and plugged it in by the bedside table.

Then I had a shower and washed my hair. There was an assortment of white towels hanging over a rail. They had all been folded uniformly with sharp right-angled corners. I took just one to dry myself with. When I'd combed my wet hair back off my face I looked in the long mirror.

I had a small frame and was thin, too thin perhaps.

I had tiny breasts. I hardly needed to wear a bra, but I did.

Even with no clothes on I looked young. I used one arm to cover my breasts and the other hand to cover my pubic hair. With no make-up on I looked just a child. I was seventeen but it seemed that my body would never catch up with my age. I put on my underwear, then pulled on the jeans I had been wearing the night before. I peeled the sticker off one of the vest tops and put it on.

I picked up my phone. There was a text from Patrice.

**Just been round yours. Your mum says you've gone away! You're staying with a friend! Who???
Just let me know** ☹

Patrice would be astonished to see me here.

She would be *desperate* to know how this situation came about.

I wished I could ring, tell her. I wished I could invite her to come. I imagined myself saying to Harry, *This is my best friend, Patrice. And Patrice, this is Dom, Harry's friend, and his girlfriend, Suzie.* But I knew that if Patrice came then I would slide into the shadows. She would become the centre of attention because that's how it was with her. People liked her. They liked to look at her, to talk to her, to listen to what she had to say. She was funny and quick-witted. She would steal the limelight wherever she went. She would have taken a firm hand with Harry. After three kisses she would have made things move on. She had courage I did not.

I put my phone down and walked out into the living room. I had to be more forward. I had to take control of this situation. Tomorrow I would most certainly go home, and I wanted to make the most of this weird and wonderful day.

I could smell the pizzas cooking. On the work surface was a bottle of beer and an opener beside it. Harry was out on the balcony talking to someone on his mobile. I opened the beer and took a swig. I was thirsty, no doubt from the beers I'd drunk in the afternoon.

I looked at Harry from behind and something seemed to scamper across my chest. I wanted him. It wasn't a feeling I had experienced before. Benji Ashe had been completely different. I had gone with him because he was convenient. I honestly hadn't thought much about it. At the time I'd assumed it was the same for him, that we'd both been handy for each other. I remembered the birthday card he'd sent me the day before though. It was probably still among the stuff in my bag. I wondered if he was just being polite about my birthday or whether our brief fling had meant more to him than it had to me.

I could hear Harry talking on the phone. I was about to walk across and tap his shoulder to let him know I was there when I heard him mention my name.

'Stacey is really sweet. She's nice. I like her.'

I moved back behind the wall of the kitchen so that he didn't see me there and feel embarrassed that I had heard him

93

talking about me. I listened. His voice was soft, tentative, as if he was talking to someone he knew very well.

'I know I said that, but she's had some trouble at home. She's on her own. I'm looking after her. You said that was the right thing to do.'

It was odd to hear myself being discussed. I wanted to say, *You don't need to look after me!* But actually I liked the fact that he was taking care of me. I had exaggerated running away from home, but he didn't know that.

He hadn't spoken for a few moments. He was listening. I peeked out and could see him walking up and down on the balcony.

'Marty, I know what I said but . . .'

His tone had changed. It was more guarded now. I sensed that he wasn't happy. Perhaps Marty hadn't liked the look of me. Possibly he'd regretted saying I could stay there. Or maybe it was deeper than that. Harry was a rich boy from Fulham and I was a girl from the East End. It sounded good for the plot of a romance novel but not in real life. It was mad. No doubt his brother wanted someone better for him.

'She says she's seventeen but she doesn't look it . . .'

His brother thinks I'm an underage runaway.

'This isn't fair, Marty. I like her. She's different . . .'

I wondered who it was that I was different from. Maybe it was Melanie, the girl with the red hair and the black jeep.

'Tomorrow? I don't know . . .'

There was a buzzing sound, loud, raucous. It made me jump and I looked towards the front door of the apartment.

'I have to go. Dom and Suzie are here.'

He ended the call. He didn't move for a few moments. I didn't want to look out in case he saw and knew that I'd been there the whole time. Then I heard him walk across the living room and pick up an entry phone from a small screen by the door. I could see faces on the screen.

'Hiya. I'll buzz you in,' he said.

I walked out of the kitchen and into the living room. I was remembering what he'd said about me to his brother. I was bursting with emotion. He had stuck up for me. He turned and smiled and was about to speak when I walked up to him and threaded my arms around his waist and went on tiptoes to kiss him. I did it slowly, my tongue touching his mouth, my hands firmly around his back.

He was surprised. Then he kissed me back, gently at first and then harder.

I wanted to pull him towards the sofa or into the bedroom but we were interrupted by a knocking on the door. It was Dom and Suzie. I stepped back away from him. My skin was hot, my breasts aching. It would have to wait until later, after they had gone.

Fourteen

When Dom and Suzie walked into the apartment they were in the middle of a conversation. It sounded like an argument.

'So, tell your mum you don't want to go!'

'I can't,' Dom said. 'You know what she's like, she'll threaten my allowance.'

Dom was still dressed like a beach bum. He paused when he saw me.

'Suzie, this is Stacey who I told you about. Stacey, Suzie . . .'

Suzie was taller than me and had long, straight black hair parted in the middle. She was wearing a tight black skirt and plimsolls. Over the top was a white baggy T-shirt that she'd tied in a knot at one side.

'Hiya, Stacey.'

Her outfit was interesting. If I'd been in a cafe and she'd been walking past I might have sketched her.

The two of them headed for the sofa and sprawled out. They'd obviously been to the apartment before and felt at home there. Harry joined them. For a while there was a three-way conversation about people they all knew. I sat on a stool and leaned back against the wall. From time to time Suzie looked at different bits of me and was seemingly unable to keep a frown off her face.

We ate pizzas and watched clips from YouTube on the television screen. After a while Dom got out a tobacco roll. He placed it on the coffee table, opened it and began to roll up two cigarettes. Inside the packet was a tiny plastic bag of dope. Dom took pinches of it out and pushed it into the roll-ups. He licked the paper and pinched the ends. Then he lit one and handed it to Harry. Harry inhaled it and offered it to me but I shook my head. I'd tried dope once before and it had made me cough. Suzie said, *No thanks*, sharply before it came her way. Dom started talking about a vintage Lambretta he liked and was definitely going to get depending on his A-level grades the following year – *if my mum allows it*. This went on for ages until Harry got out a couple of sets of headphones and he and Dom started to play war games.

Suzie watched it all without a word and from time to time drank from a bottle of Diet Coke, which she kept by her side, unscrewing the top and then screwing it back tightly when she was finished. It was as if she thought someone might grab a swig while she wasn't looking. After a while she and I took the plates back to the kitchen. I tried to start a conversation.

'Where do you go to school?'

Under the kitchen lights I could see that the roots of her hair were lighter and that her hair was dyed black.

'City of London Girls.'

'Sixth form?'

'Lower sixth. Doing four A levels. Applying for medicine next year. Don't know if I'll get in but . . .'

'A doctor?'

'My dad's a surgeon. My mum's a psychiatrist. It's the family business.'

There was a silence. She finally realised that it was polite to return the enquiry.

'You?'

'My school's in Stratford.'

'Oh, nice. You can see some of the plays.'

'No, Stratford. East London. Where the Olympics were.'

I was waiting for her to say *atte-Bowe*, but she didn't.

'Cool,' she said, and unscrewed the Coke bottle, took a drink from it, then screwed the lid back on as tight as it would go.

'I'm thinking of going to the London College of Fashion. I'm interested in designing . . .'

'I know a girl who went there. A friend of my sister's. She works for Stella McCartney now. I say she *works* for her. She's an intern. Doesn't get paid a penny but her dad supports her, so it's all good experience.'

'That sounds great,' I said.

She stared at me for a few minutes and then did a half-laugh as though something she'd thought about had amused her.

'What?' I said, feeling a bit irked.

'Nothing.'

'No, go on. Say what you're thinking.'

She shrugged. 'It's just that . . . you're *so* like Harry's last girlfriend.'

'You mean Melanie?' I said, puzzled.

'No, she was yonks ago. No, I mean Bella from the Oxfam shop in Shoreditch. She was like you. I don't mean that in an insulting way. She was lovely. But you and her do have one thing in common.'

There was a pause in which I was supposed to say, *What? What do we have in common?* But I didn't want to ask her what she meant. I didn't want to give her the pleasure. I knew she was baiting me and I decided I didn't like her, not one bit. I turned on the hot water and concentrated on the mixer tap. I thought about Bella from the Oxfam shop. I was confused. I'd thought that Harry had still been in love with Melanie. Who was Bella? I turned back to Suzie.

'Anyway, I'm not his girlfriend,' I said. 'He's just letting me stay here tonight. That's all.'

'Cool. It's just that you look his *type*.'

I bridled. I wasn't a type. I was me.

'I mean you look *young*. So did Bella.'

I turned my back to her and began to wash the plates, holding them under the stream of hot water. After a few moments she gave a long-suffering sigh and went back into the living room.

I wished that she and Dom would go.

I went back into the room where my stuff was. No one came after me. No one missed me, it seemed. I suddenly felt despondent. I sat on the bed and picked up the brochure that I'd got from the London College of Fashion that morning and looked through. There was a whole range of BA courses in fashion: Bespoke Tailoring, Fashion Contour, Fashion Design and Development, Fashion Pattern Cutting, Fashion Design Technology and others. For the first time I felt a little out of my depth. Who was I kidding? Was I going to go to college and be able to study one of these very specific courses when all I did was sketch clothes in my book? I'd have A levels – Art, English and Sociology – but would any of those equip me for a course like this? Was it just a stupid dream? I let the brochure drop. I'd been so pleased to get it earlier in the day, but now it felt like a door closing in my face. I wished I hadn't looked at it.

On the bed, underneath one of my folders, I saw the edge of the pattern that had fallen out of the book that Patrice had bought for me. I picked it up. Across the top was the word *BUTTERICK* and underneath was a drawing of a woman in a wedding dress. It was long with a kick pleat at the back and lace sleeves that went right down to the fingers. There was a back and front view and the style seemed to be from the 1960s or 1970s. I put my hand inside and riffled through the tissue-paper pattern. I pulled it out. It had yellowed and was crinkly and torn in places, as if it had been well used.

The image of the woman in the wedding dress was a line drawing with colour. It reminded me of the way I sketched the clothes I saw on people that I liked. Someone had seen this pattern and thought it would make a lovely wedding dress. They'd bought it. They'd selected fabric and zips, buttons and trims. They'd either made it for themselves or paid a dressmaker to make it – perhaps the person who had once owned the book *Twentieth-Century Style*.

Wasn't that, in the end, what being a dress designer was all about? Having a vision of a garment that would suit the needs of someone else, that would give enormous pleasure to the wearer? I picked up my sketchbook and flicked it open. I turned to the pages where I'd drawn out some original designs. I placed the Butterick pattern next to one of them. Mine wasn't a wedding dress but the image wasn't so different. I could do a job like that. I'd need to be taught masses of stuff but I *could* do it.

The sound of music was coming from the living room and I assumed Harry and Dom had finished their games.

I tidied some of my things back into my bag and picked up the card that Harry had given me. How odd to have such a thing; it reminded me of a period drama on television where men in top hats went visiting and left their cards on silver trays. This one was personalised though, because he'd drawn a heart on it. The pen strokes were uneven and the lines didn't quite meet, but it had been done just as he was leaving – a message to me. He wanted me to know that he *liked* me. He'd left me spinning on the pavement, watching the taxi drive away. I was still dizzied by it all.

I stood up, feeling better. Why was I getting upset about everything? I wasn't going to let sulky Suzie spoil it for me. So what if Harry had seen someone else after Melanie?

There was a knock and the door opened.

'You OK?' Harry said. 'The others are going.'

I was pleased but tried not to show it. I walked back into the living room. Dom was already out of the door and Harry followed him into the corridor. Suzie hung back though.

'Just a bit of advice,' she said, in a low voice. 'Be careful with that one. He's done some bad things with girls.'

I was taken aback. She was supposed to be Harry's friend. Why would she say that to me, a stranger? I didn't know what to say. She walked off without another word. Dom glanced back at me and I realised then that apart from saying hello he hadn't spoken to me at all. I didn't like either of them. They walked towards the lift without speaking to each other or touching.

Fifteen

It was almost midnight. Harry seemed unsteady on his feet. The smell of dope was sickly and sweet. The room looked messy. The sofa cushions had been discarded and lay untidily on the carpet. The headphones had been left on the seat and there were beer bottles on the coffee table.

'I'm going to take a shower,' Harry said.

'OK. I'll just . . .'

The bathroom door closed before I could finish. I tidied up and put the bottles on the kitchen worktop and replaced the headphones in a cupboard by the speakers. I could hear the shower running and wondered if Harry was all right. I hadn't spoken to him, not really, since the phone call he'd had with his brother earlier in the evening.

I walked towards the glass doors and stepped outside onto the balcony. The darkness was dotted with twinkling lights. It was warm and nice to feel the air on my arms and shoulders. I sat on a cane chair and looked over the edge. Below me the city was busy. Even though it was almost twelve there was movement and traffic and it made me feel relaxed. After a stilted couple of hours with Dom and Suzie, it was nice to hear life going on as normal. After a while I heard the bathroom door open and shut. Moments later Harry appeared in the kitchen with a towel around his waist. He opened the fridge and took out a beer, waved at me and went into his bedroom.

My skin tingled with the cool night air. I rubbed the tops of my arms. How was it possible to have such powerful feelings for someone when you'd only just met them? The cliché *Love at first sight* came into my mind, but that hadn't happened. I hadn't had a rush of emotion when I first looked at him. It was when we were talking, when he was finding out about me, when I was finding out about him. When he said, *I thought I was in love with this girl* . . . Those words gave him stature. He was capable of doing something reckless for love and it had knocked me over. All day I'd been trying to get up again, but I couldn't.

And now there was this girl Bella to think about. She was like me, Suzie had said. Did that make me feel upset? Or pleased? Or just plain jealous that someone else had been around since Melanie? Had I thought that I was the only one?

I wanted him. I knew that with absolute certainty. We'd kissed four times and each time I'd been hungry for more. I wanted to feel his skin and put my fingers in his damp hair. I got up and walked back into the living room. I went to his room door and tapped on it lightly. I opened it and found him sitting on the end of the bed in his boxer shorts. On the carpet, by his feet, were the towels he'd used. I felt myself falter but thought about Patrice. If she'd desired Harry, she would have had him. Why couldn't I be like her for once?

'You OK?' he asked sleepily.

I steeled myself and went across to the bed and sat down beside him.

I put one arm around his shoulder. I touched his chin with my other hand and turned his face so that I could kiss him. He didn't seem to respond for a few moments and I wondered if I'd got it completely wrong. But then he moved his hand around my back and began to kiss me intently. I ran my fingers down his chest and felt this lurch inside my stomach. I took his hand and I guided it to my breast and he dropped back onto the bed, taking me with him. I lay on my side, my skin alight. The duvet was rumpled beneath us and I rolled so that I was half on top of him, my leg across his stomach. I felt him stiffen and kissed him harder. I wanted this.

But he stopped and rolled away from me.

He sat up. His eyes looked woozy.

'I can't. You're a guest. I'd be taking advantage. I just can't.'

'No, you wouldn't! This is what I want,' I said, running my hand across his chest, feeling the softness of the hairs on his skin.

'I like you, Stacey, but I just can't. It's too soon.'

'But it's not too soon if we want to. I have condoms in my bag.'

His face broke into a smile. He lay back down on the bed, his elbow holding his head up. But I slumped back, puzzled, confused. What about the kiss on the escalator? In the taxi? In the lift?

He put his middle finger on my throat and ran it down onto my vest, between my breasts and onto my jeans, stopping above my groin.

'You're so sweet and I'd like to – don't think I wouldn't – but . . .'

I took his hand and pulled it gently downwards.

'I'm not a virgin,' I whispered. 'I've done this before.'

He sat up.

'I'm flattered but . . .'

I was confused. I'd made a fool of myself. I sat up. I went to stand up but he had my hand, pulling me back down.

'Stacey, there's no need to rush. I *like* you. Let's just take our time,' he said.

This wasn't the way things were meant to happen.

'Stacey,' he said, his lips at my ear.

I turned to him and he kissed my mouth and put his fingers in my hair.

'Just take it slowly,' he said. 'You go and have a good night's sleep.'

I nodded. When I left his room I felt confused. I walked across the living room and shut the balcony door and headed for my room. What had just happened? He could have had sex with me. Most of the boys I knew wouldn't have stopped, and yet he did.

It was mad but it made me want him more than I had before.

Sixteen

I woke up just after nine. The apartment was quiet. I hadn't closed the blinds before going to bed so the room was blazing with sunlight. I'd also left a window open so I could hear the sound of the traffic from down below in the street. I listened through the cars and lorries and beeps to see if there was any movement in the apartment, but there wasn't. Harry was still asleep in the next bedroom. I threw off the cover and lay there in the yellow haze and thought about the night before.

I should have felt mortified but I didn't. I had offered myself to Harry and he had turned me down. I had tried to persuade him. *I'm not a virgin*, I'd said.

It was what I'd wanted to do. After a day of falling for him I'd wanted to show my feelings in that raw way. No tiptoeing around it. I'd wanted my body to tell him how I felt, but he had backed off. *There's no need to rush, I like you*, he'd said. Those words had thrown me at first, but thinking about them over and over I realised they implied a *future*. That the whirlwind day I'd had yesterday wasn't just for one day. There would be more. All I had to do was wait.

Well, I could wait.

I picked up my phone and saw that I had a message from my dad.

Back from Corfu. Saw that you stayed the night
so I rang your mum. Everything all right?
She's says there was a row. Come round
and see us if you want xxxx

Come round and see *us*. Now whenever I wanted to spend time with dad Gemma was likely to be there.

No, I'm fine. Going home tonight.
Maybe see you at the weekend xx

Once I'd sent it I realised that I was going to go home that day.

Two nights away was long enough to make a point. I couldn't miss any more school. At that very moment I should have been in double Art. I would have been working on my textile design and later, if I had time, I would have done some preparation for my portfolio on lens-based photography. I was busy and really shouldn't have missed the session, especially if I was going to apply for the London College of Fashion in the autumn.

I got dressed and took the brochure and my sketchpad and some notepaper out to the kitchen. I placed them on the table and then sat down and looked closely at the course descriptions. I underlined some stuff and drew asterisks where I wanted to look again. I knew I'd need to search for details on the website, maybe even ring up for more information.

I was feeling hungry. I looked around to see if there was any food for breakfast. The fridge was empty except for some bottles of beer and white wine. In a cupboard I found some teabags, so I made black tea and sat down at the table and drank it. Then I started sketching, just freehand, making shapes of skirts, tops and jackets. After I'd finished two rough designs I realised I'd given the figure a ponytail that hung long and straight down her back.

Patrice was never far from my mind. I should text her. The trouble was I had so much to say; so many things had happened. How could I fit it all into the screen of my phone? It would be better if I went to see her *as soon* as I got home that evening. Then I could tell her about seeing Shelly and being upset, but that would be balanced with all the new stuff I had to tell her. She might even end up feeling envious of *me* and the things that had been happening in *my* life.

I flipped back through the pages of my pad and saw the drawing of the Whistles dress that I'd done the previous day. I remembered the chiffon and the black-and-white abstract design. Maybe it would also have been good in an old English Rose print, hinting at the past. It could even have been a top over tight leggings or possibly wide trousers in black silk.

The door opened behind me and I looked round and saw Harry standing there. He'd put on his shorts and T-shirt but had bare feet.

'Hiya,' he said.

'Hi.'

I didn't feel awkward or shy. I looked back at my pad and wrote some notes at the bottom of the sketch. He walked past me towards the fridge, opened it and groaned.

'Should have got some milk and eggs. I never thought.'

'There are teabags,' I said.

He turned back and looked down at my sketchpad.

'What's this? A design?'

'No, it's a dress I saw in Selfridges yesterday. I just liked it so I sketched it.'

'Melanie wore Whistles clothes.'

He sat down. I could feel his bare arm next to mine. His skin was cool.

'I'm not going to stay tonight,' I said. 'I've decided to go home and face the family, try to sort things out.'

'You sure?'

'This is a good time to go back. Thanks for letting me stay.'

'You're not going to go now though? I thought we could hang out today.'

'This afternoon.'

'That's good.'

'I was thinking, maybe, when I go home, you could contact me. We could meet up.'

'Course I will,' he said.

He was flicking through my brochure. There was something in the way he said it that made me feel uneasy. It was too quick, thoughtless. I wondered, for the first time, what he really felt. I flicked to a fresh page and wrote out my name and address. I tore it out and gave it to him.

'Here, so that you know where to find me.'

He placed it on the table.

'Is this the college you want to go to?'

I nodded. He closed the brochure and leaned across and kissed me on the cheek. At the same time he put his arm around me, his fingers playing with the strap of my vest, fiddling with it so that it fell off my shoulder. Then his hand slipped under my arm and touched the edge of my breast. I held my breath, feeling his fingers pressing my flesh. I turned to him, my mouth slightly open. I wanted to kiss him but he just smiled and pulled his hand back.

'Let's go out to eat. There's a breakfast bar in Selfridges and I have my brother's account card. I'm hungry. In any case, if I stay here with you I might do something I'll regret.'

He stood up, picking up the page with my address on it. He folded it once, then again, and put it into his shorts pocket.

I watched him go. *I wouldn't regret it*, I thought.

Breakfast was in a restaurant at the top of Selfridges. It was a long glass conservatory with a bar and tables perched on the top of the giant store. There were a number of men in suits and well-dressed shoppers, but Harry, wearing T-shirt, shorts and trainers, just walked up to the man at the entrance and said, 'Table for two, please,' with gusto, as though he went there regularly. While we were eating (scrambled eggs for me and omelette for him, plus orange juices) he told me that his brother had taken him there many times. When the bill came Harry gave the waiter a card and then he had to sign for it. I didn't look to see how much it was. I was just in awe at being in such a glamorous place.

We went walking through the store. Harry seemed a little preoccupied and kept looking at his phone.

'What's up?' I said.

'Dom keeps texting. He's in a bad place right now. He's had a row with his dad and he and Suzie have split up again. They

111

split up every couple of weeks but then they get back together. I've told him to come back to the apartment. That OK?'

I shrugged. It wasn't anything to do with me.

'He says he'll come about two. I'll have to go back and let him in.'

'I'll be packing my stuff anyway.'

We were walking around the men's fashions and he'd been looking at some shirts and jeans when he got a call. I wondered if it was Dom again.

'I have to take this,' he said.

He walked away from me and I thought, for a moment, that it might be Melanie. Was it really over between him and her? Or could it be Bella, the girl from the charity shop in Shoreditch? He was talking quickly though, and looked pained. Possibly it was Dom again or his brother. It could have been his mother demanding to know where he was. After a few moments more the call ended and he came walking back to me.

'I've had an idea,' he said. 'Let's go upstairs.'

'Everything all right?' I said.

He mumbled something and led me towards the women's fashions. He walked purposefully along as though he knew where he was heading. We'd just used the escalator and I'd stood on the stair ahead of him and turned round the way I'd done the day before when he'd first kissed me. I'd hoped he'd recall it but he was looking away, his phone still welded to his hand. I was disappointed. He was preoccupied. That kiss was something I would always remember, but maybe it would be better if we went back to the apartment and I got my stuff and went home.

We stopped at the Whistles collection.

The dress I had drawn was still hanging in the same place. He pointed it out.

'See if they've got your size,' he said.

'Why?'

'Just see. Try it on. Why not? We've got time.'

I looked at the rail and saw three of the dresses at the far end. I found my size.

'It would probably be too long for me anyway. Dresses always are,' I said.

'Try it on.'

I felt embarrassed but I picked up the dress. An assistant came scurrying over. She was tall and thin, with frizzy black hair and glasses that had white frames.

'Can I help?' she said, looking at me a little suspiciously.

'My girlfriend is just trying on this dress,' Harry said.

Harry's accent and his tone reassured her. She didn't falter. She gave a gracious smile and pointed to the changing room. I walked past her without a look. *My girlfriend*, he had said. It was mad. Inside I took the dress off its hanger and slipped it over my head. I let it slither down my body before I wriggled out of my jeans.

It was a perfect fit. It stopped just under my knee. It would be better worn with high heels, but maybe flat sandals would be OK. There was a mirror behind me and I angled myself so that I could see the back.

It was lovely, something I would never be able to afford.

I peeked out of the changing area. Harry was there, for once not looking at his phone.

'That's really nice,' he said.

'It is. I'll just get changed again.'

I took it off reluctantly. I looked at the price and gasped: £190. I put it back on the hanger and got dressed again. I carried it out with me. The assistant took it from my hands very politely.

'Come on,' Harry said, and we began to follow her towards the cash register.

She stood behind the counter and laid the dress out on top of tissue paper. Harry handed her a card and I realised then what he was doing.

'No!' I said. 'No, you can't. I can't accept it. Really . . .'

He came close to me. 'It's a gift. I can afford it and it makes me happy to give it to you.'

'But it's your brother's card.'

'He gives me an allowance. If I don't spend it, he'll think I don't need it.'

'I don't know what to say.'

'Well, I don't know what they say in Stratford-atte-Bowe, but in Fulham we say thank you if someone gives us a present.'

'Thank you,' I said.

The assistant looked at me with a smile and gave me the bag that held the dress – the most expensive thing I had ever owned.

Seventeen

Dom was waiting outside Poole Place. He had his back against the wall and barely glanced at us as we walked towards him. His stance looked deliberate, as if he was posing for a photograph.

We'd been in a pub drinking beers and I'd had more than I'd wanted and was feeling a little lightheaded. Harry had drunk some shots with his beers but seemed sober. I had my Selfridges bag in my hand, my fingers gripping the handles, as if someone might come along and wrest it off me.

'Hiya,' Harry said when we got to the entrance of the apartments.

Dom sighed long and loud. He looked different. He was wearing jeans and trainers and a football shirt. The beach bum look I'd seen the day before had gone. There were no beads or flip-flops.

'Are you a fan?' I said, surprised.

'Chelsea. Too true.'

Harry entered the code and we walked into the building. We all rode up in the lift in silence. Harry didn't ask Dom about the row with his parents and the fact that he'd broken up with Suzie. I noticed that Dom had a bag with him and I heard the

115

clink of glass. Once in the apartment he put a bottle of vodka and a bottle of soda water on the kitchen worktop. He also took out the tobacco roll that he'd had the previous night. It looked fatter than before. Harry smiled when he saw it.

'Got any ice?' Dom said.

'I think so.'

'I'm sorry you've broken up with Suzie,' I said, feeling I ought to say something.

'I'm not!'

'Don't give him any sympathy,' Harry said lightly. 'He likes to feel sorry for himself.'

Dom put a finger up at Harry and filled a glass with ice.

'All right if I play a game?' he said, gesturing towards the living room. 'I'll keep out of your way.'

Harry nodded. 'You don't have to keep out of anyone's way.'

Dom picked up his glass and tobacco roll and went into the other room.

'He's in a mood,' I said, stating the obvious.

'He's always like this when he and Suzie break up. And his dad's a bastard.'

'Oh.'

'Knocks him about. He's spent more time in my house than his.'

'Can't he go to the police?'

'You don't do that when it's family. You just don't. You put up with it.'

I must have had some odd kind of expression on my face.

'Stacey, you're not the only one with family troubles. If it wasn't for my brother, I'd have left home years ago.'

'But you have so much. And your schooling. You've got so much to look forward to . . .'

'I know. I'm a poor little rich boy.'

'I didn't mean it like that.'

'I'm just saying. What goes on inside families isn't simple. No matter how much money you've got.'

'I think I should shut up.'

He smiled. 'I'll keep Dom company for a while. Have a smoke. You OK on your own?'

'Course. I'm fine.'

I went into my room and began to sort out things and repack my bag. It was gone two and I hadn't intended to go home until about four, but maybe it would be best if I shot off now and left Dom and Harry alone.

On the bed was the Selfridges bag; inside was my new dress, wrapped up in tissue paper. All the way back from the shop I'd been feeling overwhelmed by the gift. Harry had been quiet though, and I wondered if he'd regretted buying it and whether his brother would be angry with him. Or maybe he'd done it to get back at his brother. The phone call the previous evening had sounded like a row of some sort, as if his brother was telling him not to get involved with me. Was this Harry's way of saying, *Mind your own business!* Did the gift of the dress mean anything to him other than spending some money on me? Money that wasn't even his. Money that he appeared to have in abundance.

I thought of Patrice and imagined her standing with her hands on her hips, berating me. *For God's sake, Stacey, it's a gift from someone who likes you, who's helped you out, who didn't try to have sex with you when he had the chance. Can't you just be pleased with it?*

And she would be right. Why did I try to turn something nice into something unpleasant? He liked me. How many times did I have to try to persuade myself that it was true?

I packed and then lay back on the bed. The beers had made me feel tired. I picked up the remote and turned on the television. I flicked around the channels for a while and watched a bit of a film I'd seen before. I felt myself getting sleepy, so I turned over and put my face into the pillow and closed my eyes.

When I woke up the television was off and Harry was on the bed beside me, fast asleep. I was slightly dazed and had to think for a minute where I was. I sat up and looked at my phone. It was 3.35 p.m. I'd slept for more than an hour. My head felt heavy. I'd drunk too much at lunchtime. I'd had too many drinks for a girl who hardly drank at all (except for some freezing-cold white wine with Patrice now and then).

I gazed at Harry. Had he come into the room because he wanted to be with me? I put my fingers on his arm but he didn't move. He looked completely out of it. He'd been smoking dope as well as drinking.

I was touched that he had come in to see me.

There were sounds coming from the living room. I got up and went to the door and opened it. Dom was sitting on the sofa, wearing a headset and holding a control pad. On the screen was a war game – tanks and planes and ridiculous-looking soldiers. There was no sound coming from it but every few seconds Dom made a *Yes!* or *Whoa!* or swore. It was frenetic.

I wondered how Dom had the energy, as he'd been smoking dope as well.

I went back into the bedroom and decided to have a shower to wake myself up. Then I would get dressed and go. This two-day odyssey of mine would be over. The truth was I was a little tired of it. The best bit of it was the time I'd spent with Harry. I'd be quite happy if I never saw Dom or Suzie ever again.

The shower got rid of the sluggishness I felt. I used the same towel I'd used the previous night to dry myself and put on my underwear. Then I covered up with another towel and went back into the bedroom and found Harry awake. He was lying staring at me, his hands behind his head. His eyes looked a little intense from the dope. I went across to the bed and sat down beside him.

'I'm going to go home now.'

He put his hand up and touched my arm.

'You're not rushing off because Dom is here?'

'No, I was going to go anyway. Remember, I said?'

He nodded but pulled my arm towards him. I leaned across and kissed him.

'You smell good,' he said.

I backed away, intending to finish dressing. He held onto me though. His eyes looked drunk and he slightly slurred when he spoke.

'Come and lie down with me for a while.'

'I can't,' I said, pointing to the door of the room.

'He doesn't care. He's busy. Come on, before you go home. Last night ...'

The night before I had offered myself, had said I wasn't a virgin, had mentioned my pack of condoms. But today seemed different; the time didn't feel right. Last night we'd been alone. Now there was company.

'Just lie down for a cuddle. We don't have to do anything.'

'Not with him out there . . .'

'He's preoccupied. Come on, Stacey. Just five minutes. Take this off.'

He pulled at the towel that was around me. I stood up and let it drop off. I only had on my pants and bra and his eyes travelled up and down my body. Instead of feeling embarrassed, trying to cover myself up, I stood still and let him look at me. Then I walked slowly around the bottom of the bed and sat down on the other side, shifting into a lying position next to him.

Just five minutes, then I would get dressed and go.

He kissed me on the mouth. I turned my head to make it easier and felt his lips, slippery and impatient. His arms pulled me tightly towards him and his fingers slipped up the back of my bra. It was just supposed to be a few kisses and yet I felt myself moving like liquid around him, my legs twisting over him, my arm up and down his back. My eyes were tightly closed, a searing feeling radiating through me. I felt his stiffness and it gave me a quickening in my groin and I knew that this wasn't going to be just a few kisses.

There were still sounds from outside, the *Ohs* and *Ahs* of the war game.

'I want this,' I whispered.

I undid my bra and pulled it off. I could feel his skin against my breasts. There was a voice in the back of my head that said,

Condoms, but I ignored it. I pushed myself up against him and felt lightheaded and tingling with pleasure. The room seemed to sink away and it was just the two of us, slipping and sliding together on the bed. I wanted to do it. I wanted to go all the way with this boy who had scooped me up out of Shoreditch and brought me here.

I pulled at the zip on his shorts. I tugged at the top button. I was ready. He was ready. Then I heard something that seemed to come from far away.

The room door opened.

It took me a moment to register it. I opened my eyes but I continued kissing him. I was like a car that couldn't suddenly stop. I eventually pulled my mouth away and saw someone standing at the door.

It was Marty, Harry's brother.

Eighteen

Marty was standing at the door of the bedroom. I was startled, embarrassed. I pushed myself up to a sitting position and put my arm across my breasts to hide my nakedness. His brother had allowed me to stay in the flat; had he also considered that this might happen? Would he be angry? Would Harry be in trouble? I couldn't read his face. I didn't know him. I'd only seen him once from inside a taxi.

'It's all right, Stacey. Marty is cool,' Harry said, his voice husky.

His brother didn't mind what Harry did; maybe he even sanctioned it. Harry in bed with a girl . . . this was what boys did.

I had my eyes on Marty's face, but I couldn't read his expression.

He was staring at *me*, not at Harry. I remembered the phone call the previous evening when Harry had seemed to be arguing with him about me. Was Marty *cool* with his brother having sex with girlfriends, but maybe, for some reason, he didn't approve of me?

'I'm sorry,' I said.

Marty smiled and walked towards the bed.

'You are sweet, Stacey,' he replied. 'Just like Harry said.'

I sat up completely, confused. I felt exposed and pulled at the sheet to try to cover myself up, but it was underneath both of us and I couldn't get it to move. I bent my knees so that they were in front of me. The room seemed chilled and my skin rose up in goosebumps. Harry was still lying at my side and I felt his lips on my arm, kissing my skin.

'It's OK, Stacey. This is my brother. It's fine. It's not a problem,' he said.

Marty sat down on the end of the bed.

'You had your gift. Your dress? Harry says you looked great in it.'

I frowned.

'Maybe you could try it on later,' Marty said.

I felt Harry's hand running up my leg towards my knee. His brother was watching.

'You don't need to hide your breasts, Stacey,' he said.

He took his jacket off and let it fall to the floor. A terrible feeling was creeping over me. I felt Harry at my side. His body was hot and he was propped up on his elbow, close to me. I looked back to his brother. I could see his shirtsleeves were rolled back, the way they had been the previous afternoon. He pulled at the knot of his tie and it loosened and he took it off over his neck. For a second it looked like a noose. Then he dropped it on the ground.

'You should go,' I said, as politely as I could. 'I have to get dressed.'

'No, no. You look sweeter like that.'

I moved my legs to get up off the bed but Harry was holding them, making shushing sounds, then kissing my shoulder.

'This'll be good,' he whispered.

I knew then what was going to happen. A sick feeling weighed down my stomach. I made a sudden twist as if to throw Harry off but he was bigger than me, stronger, more forceful. He wasn't hurting me, but I couldn't get off the bed.

'Come on, Stacey. It's not like you're a virgin,' Harry whispered.

I looked at him and felt a pain in my chest like a needle forcing its way through my heart. Had this been what it was all about? At the end of the bed Marty had stood up and was undoing the belt on his trousers. He unzipped them and let them drop to the floor. I heard money chinking in the pockets as they fell at his feet. His belt was thick, heavy leather and it stayed in the loops.

'No, Harry,' I said, shaking my head at him. 'I don't want this. No, no, no . . .'

Harry had his arm around my shoulders and was holding me in one place. He was shushing me, his leg across mine. Then Marty sat on the bed. He still had his boxer shorts on and his shirt was done up, his stomach straining through it. I was afraid, like a trapped animal. I tried to move, to push Harry's leg away, but it was clamped on mine. He kept kissing my face and I kept wiping it away.

'He's my brother, Stacey. He does everything for me.'

I stared at him as if he was a stranger, a boy who had snatched me off the street. And in that moment I knew the truth: *he was a stranger*. I just hadn't known it.

'Come on, sweetie,' I heard his brother say. 'We're just going to have some fun, that's all.'

A hand grabbed each of my ankles and hauled me down the bed. I shook my head at Harry but his eyes were deep and drowsy. I felt fingers take one side of my pants and pull them all the way down my leg, tugging them over my knees and ankles, until they were off. Harry seemed to roll away then. He let go of me and I felt the weight of Marty on my legs, on my stomach, on my chest.

'NO! NO!' I spluttered.

I was like a swimmer, overwhelmed by water.

One of Marty's hands edged my legs apart and I felt his penis pushing at me. My muscles went rigid as if to hold him out, to stop him forcing himself inside. My hands were in fists, squashed against my chest. Marty's shirt was in my face and I could smell nicotine. I was flat against the mattress, pinned down. I seemed to hold my breath to stop myself drowning. I could feel his hand fumbling, his knuckles digging into the sides of my thighs, as he shoved his penis into me.

He made a moaning sound.

It hurt me. I felt my voice catch in my throat but no words came out.

'Relax, relax,' he said, moving backwards and forwards.

My stomach rose up to my mouth. I was rigid, a tiny girl under a tank of a man. I glanced up at him and saw that his eyes were closed and his face was screwed up as if he was in a trance.

'So sweet, Stacey,' he whispered.

I closed my eyes and put myself in a dark room, the door locked so no one could get in. Somewhere that I thought was

126

safe. From far away I could feel him moving faster, backwards and forwards, and then he shouted out and stopped. His back stiffened and I felt all his weight on my groin. I opened my eyes and looked at his hateful face and felt myself crushed and broken. He seemed to deflate and all his weight settled on me. My mouth opened and I made a wailing sound and used my fists to try to push him off. His face was serene though, and then he slid off me onto the bed as if he was a hot-air balloon that had just come down to earth. I rolled away and half fell off the bed. I picked up my pants and looked around to see that Harry was gone. I went into the en-suite and locked the door.

I pulled the rest of the white towels off the rack and wound them round and round me, covering myself up. I sat on the floor trembling and started to sob.

After a long time I got up. I opened the door. I looked across to the bed and saw that Marty was still lying there. On the floor by the bed were his trousers.

He sat up when he saw me.

'Stacey, you all right?' he said, lots of concern in his voice.

I avoided looking at him. I gathered my clothes from various parts of the room and began to put them on. My bag was already packed from before so I picked it up.

He moved across the bed towards me.

I backed off. He was reaching for his trousers though. I thought he might put them on but he was feeling in the pockets and he pulled out a leather wallet. I walked towards the door.

'Wait,' he said.

He got up off the bed. His shirt hung over his boxer shorts, his legs white and thin. He held out his hand. There was money in it.

'Get a taxi home,' he said.

I shook my head angrily. He stepped towards me and pushed the money into my hand.

'It was just a bit of fun, Stacey.'

I opened the door and walked into the living room. Harry and Dom were there on the sofa. They both had headphones on and were playing war games. Neither of them looked round as I left the apartment.

Part Two

Nineteen

I didn't give my story to Patrice. It took me almost a week to write it but I couldn't quite bring myself to hand it over. It was on my laptop under the file name *Oxford Street*. Patrice had been treating me like an invalid all week, waiting for me outside lessons, coming into the library with a sneaky cereal bar and asking, 'Are you OK?' I half expected her to pull out a blanket from her bag and tuck it around my knees. She linked my arm wherever we went as though she was keeping hold of me in case I spun off to Shoreditch or Oxford Street again.

It wasn't that I didn't trust her. *She* wasn't the problem.

The story, once I'd written it and read it over a few times, was like a testament to my own stupidity. How could I have been so naive, so swept up in my own romantic daydreams, not to realise that there was a subtext to what was happening?

Why would Harry fall for someone like me?

Patrice knew the bare facts of what had happened in those couple of days, but if she read my story she would see a side of me I was ashamed of. I was gullible. I was easily led. I let my feelings smother any common sense I might have had about going to an apartment with a boy I barely knew. I thought I was falling in love; instead I was being manipulated, used.

I wrote the story for Patrice, but now I wasn't going to let her see it.

That week after it happened was a low time for me. Every time I got undressed to have a shower I stood in front of the bathroom mirror and looked at my body. It was pale and thin and looked the same as it had before the rape. I peered closely at my skin for some sign of what had happened, as if the assault might be imprinted on me. My bruises were metaphorical though. (I'd had trouble finding metaphors in poems, but I knew the truth of them now.)

I tried to be angry, but all I felt was hurt. Harry's brother had raped me and I should have been in a rage with him, but his face kept fading and it was Harry that I pictured, the memory of Harry that gave me pain. He had made me think he cared for me when all the time he was shaping me up for someone else.

The night before I finished the story I found the Whistles dress in the bottom of my wardrobe, where I had thrown it, among my shoes and trainers. It was in a heap where it had come unfolded. It had been there for over a week. I took it out and laid it on my bed. The sight of it gave me a leaden feeling because it was just advance payment for a rape.

The pleats in the chiffon were precise and neat, but now they looked sharp enough to cut me. The bodice was tightly fitted in contrast to the voluminous skirt. There was room to move, to dance, to walk, to run. I gathered the dress up to my chest and felt the softness of the fabric against my skin. No one else in school would have anything like it. It was the sort of dress I could keep in my wardrobe for ten years. I would have looked great in it.

I dropped it onto my bed and went to my sewing box and got out my scissors.

It took me a minute to make the first cut. The scissors hung in my fingers and I hesitated. Then I began to shred it. I let the scissors cut at random, in zigzag lines, straight up or diagonally. I criss-crossed and sliced my way through the bodice and in between the layers of fabric. Finally I took a swatch of it in each hand and pulled it apart. The fragments lay scattered across my bed, some of the chiffon floating restlessly.

Then there were the text messages Harry had been sending to me. There'd been four altogether, the last coming just after I finished tearing the dress apart. As if he had sensed in some way that I was imploding.

Really like you. Let's meet up again xxxx

Love to hear from you, sweet Stacey xxx

Miss you. Thinking of you xxxx

Would love to see you again xxxxxx

They were all affectionate but vague messages. I didn't believe for one minute that he meant any of them. Part of me thought that he might have regretted what happened and perhaps was trying to reach out some weird hand of friendship. When I was in a darker mood I thought he was probably sending them as electronic evidence that he had not interpreted what had happened as rape. That way, if I went to the police, he could say, *No, no, it wasn't like that. I was still texting her. I didn't think there was any problem!*

I'd deleted them all.

If only I could have deleted that day from my life.

Twenty

At school, on Friday, Patrice sent me a text to say that she was in the common room with two coffees. It was last period and we were both free. As I headed in her direction I saw Benji Ashe walking along the corridor towards me. I groaned inwardly and remembered the birthday card he'd sent to me. I had acted badly when he had been kind.

'Hi, Benji,' I said, standing still, making it clear that I was stopping to speak to him. 'Thanks for the birthday card.'

He stopped walking but stood away from me. There was enough space for a couple of year sevens to walk between us, talking loudly, nudging each other.

'I heard you weren't well. Hope you're better,' he said.

'I am.'

'I'm glad I bumped into you because I've been carrying something around with me for a while, wanting to give it back.'

'Oh?'

He rummaged in his bag and pulled out a small padded envelope that had been reused, the address crossed out and something written to the side of it. It was one of the envelopes he got his vinyl singles in.

'You left it behind in my room,' he said. 'I only found it last week when I was sorting out stuff.'

He handed the envelope to me sheepishly. I took it and put my hand inside and pulled out a flimsy scarf. It was long and narrow and I had worn it a bit like a tie, loosely round my neck. I'd made it from a bigger scarf that was too bulky. I hadn't noticed that it was gone.

'Where did you find it?'

'Under my bed,' he said, looking straight at me, his eyes latching onto mine.

I didn't know what to say. I looked down at it, letting the fine fabric slide through my fingers. It must have fallen there on one of the occasions when we'd spent time together. I tried to remember if I'd been wearing it that last day, when we'd had sex – the day when I couldn't wait to get away from him.

I felt bad.

'Thanks, I wondered where it had got to,' I said, still not looking at him and tucking the scarf back into the envelope, folding down the flap as if I was going to pop it into a post box.

'See you,' he said, and walked on.

I watched him walk away and then turned back and headed to the common room. I felt like I was going to cry. Everything that had happened to me in the last few days had made me feel emotional, on the edge of dissolving into tears. That very morning Tyler had sat up by himself in the middle of my bed. I'd let go of him and expected him to topple to the side like he usually did, but he sat there, his back straight, and smiled at me as if he knew he had done something clever. Then my mum had knocked on my room door and handed me a couple of shirts that she'd ironed on hangers. I felt overwhelmed with gratitude. Later I'd handed Tyler back to Jodie and I'd noticed that she'd washed her hair and was wearing it down around her face and looked busy. The pushchair was set up in the hall and she was on her way to a teenager and baby class that had started at the health centre. It made me feel ridiculously pleased and tearful at the same time.

I found Patrice on her own, in a corner armchair, her shoes off and her feet doubled up underneath her.

'Here's your coffee,' she said, pushing the cup towards me.

There was no one else there. The room was empty. On Friday afternoon most kids who had a free last period just went home. I sat down and sighed, wondering whether to tell her how nice Benji had been.

'Is it all right if we talk about it?' she said.

She meant the rape. I felt instantly tense.

No, not really, I wanted to say. *I'd rather we never mentioned it again.*

'I know you're still in the middle of writing your story, but I've been thinking that there are these places called Rape Crisis Centres. Maybe a chat with someone there might put your mind at rest. It's not like talking to a police officer. These people *only* deal with rapes.'

'I don't know . . .'

'Look,' Patrice said, her voice soft, 'you might not be the first person they've done this to. If you don't tell someone, if you do nothing, then Harry and his brother can do this again. Do you want some other innocent girl walking into the same thing that you did?'

137

'No.'

I thought then about the girl that Suzie had talked about, Bella, who worked in the Oxfam shop in Shoreditch. It wasn't the first time I had wondered about her. Had she been put in the same situation as me?

'So think about it tonight,' Patrice said. 'I've got the details about this centre on my laptop. We could go. I could come with you.'

'I need to finish my story first. Then I'll have it all straight in my head.'

'Good plan! Plus tomorrow you could come round mine and stay over. And I need to look at your hair. What have you done to it?' she said, making a face.

I hadn't washed it for days and I'd pulled it back in a tie so that I didn't have to think about it.

'Luckily I've got lots of product at home. I'll wash it, then we'll see . . .'

Patrice left the common room to see a teacher about an essay. I opened my laptop and searched for *Rape Crisis* on the web. The website looked very professional and was full of important and reassuring statements: *If you have been raped the most important thing to remember is that it was not your fault.* That sounded good but did it cover every single case? I read it over. Each section dealt with different aspects of the aftermath of such an assault. It looked reassuring, as if they'd tried to cover all eventualities. I read some more, glancing up from my laptop every time someone came in or went out of the common room. *Rape Crisis Centres specialise in rape trauma support and counselling.* It sounded like there'd be a lot of talking and I wasn't sure I could do that. I'd written my story. I'd poured it all out on the page and now I couldn't even bring myself to give it to my best friend. How could I talk about it to someone else?

There was another reason I couldn't go. *If you are not sure what you want to do, go along with a friend to your nearest Sexual Assault Referral Centre where you can have a forensic and medical examination.* I had no forensic evidence. My rape had happened over a week ago and I had showered and bathed more often than usual, trying to wipe away any trace of Marty Connaught from my body. I would offer no evidence except for my word.

I closed up my laptop and decided to go home. Patrice was going to be a while and I didn't feel like waiting around. She might even bring the subject up again when she came back. Just thinking about it was making me anxious, upset. I just wanted to wipe the whole thing out. Was it not possible for me to just forget about it? If I went to the police or a Rape Crisis Centre, the investigation, the trial, would eat up the next year of my life. I would spend every moment thinking about it and Marty Connaught might not even be convicted. Then I would never be able to put it out of my mind. It would be in the newspapers and even though my name would not be mentioned I would read it and know that it was me who was being discussed, my stupidity that was being examined.

I wasn't physically injured. As long as I wasn't pregnant and hadn't contracted a sexually transmitted disease, there was a possibility that I might just be able to get on with my life. If I could view it as a kind of accident, like falling down some stairs and twisting my ankle, it would hurt for a while but it would fade. Then, when it had healed, I could pretend that it had never happened. Just go on being a teenager, taking exams, looking forward to university.

Patrice wanted justice. I just wanted to ignore it.

Leave it. Forget it.

And I would have done that, honestly I would, if I hadn't walked out of school that day and seen Harry standing across the road, waiting for me.

Twenty-One

There was a black VW parked on the edge of the zigzag lines across from the main school gates. Harry was beside it. He was scanning the students coming out of the school. I saw him before he noticed me and I was able to watch for a few moments as his eyes swept from one side of the throng to the other.

He was wearing smart clothes – black trousers and a shirt, but no tie. He looked as he had that morning when I first met him in the cafe. I guessed he'd just come from school, even though he'd removed his lanyard. I stopped before the gate and gazed through the railings at him. He had a hand across his eyes to keep the sun off. His face was on the edge of a smile, as if he was holding it back until he saw me. A feeling of *longing* gripped me. Even after what he had done, I still felt the pull of him.

I wasn't entirely surprised to see him. I'd been thinking about him for days and Patrice and I had just been talking about him. It seemed almost logical that he should appear there in front of me. And there were the texts he had sent, which seemed to suggest unfinished business between us.

I stood watching him and allowed myself to feel the buzz of attraction for him. As if nothing bad had happened and I was a girl thrilled to see a boy she wanted. It wasn't until he caught sight of me and his arm went up in a tentative wave that I felt those feelings dissolve and something much more unpleasant uncurl itself in my chest. I thought of his brother then and searched the street with my eyes to see if *he* was there. Inside the black Polo I could see the profile of Dom, but there was no sign of Marty Connaught.

The number of students around me was thinning out, so I walked out of the school gates and headed away from Harry and the car.

In moments I heard him running up behind me.

'Stacey, wait!' he called.

I kept walking, my head lowered stiffly, my feet eating up the pavement one step after another. Then I felt a hand touching my arm. I stopped, spun round and took a step backwards away from him so that his hand fell from me.

'Stacey,' he said, out of breath, puffing.

I stared at him.

'You didn't answer my texts.'

I didn't speak, my eyes boring into him.

'I've come all the way here to see you. I've missed you,' he said, smiling.

I looked up the street. There were groups of students filling the bus shelters, a bit of hustling, one or two being pushed onto the road. I could hear loud shouts of indignation. I noticed the black Polo moving out onto the road, coming towards us.

'Are you at least going to say hello?'

'I didn't ask you to come here, Harry. I don't want to see you.'

'Why?'

'After what happened?'

He made a face that was half sympathetic and half incredulous.

'You didn't take any of *that* seriously. It was just a laugh. We were just chilling out. I'd smoked too much dope. You'd had a few beers. It's what people do. I thought you were cool about it . . .'

He put his hand on my arm and kept talking quickly.

'I like you. We could spend time together. If you don't want to hang around with my brother and my mates, that's fine. We can be alone.'

He was making it sound as though I didn't like his brother's company, that I was being choosy in some way.

'Your brother *raped* me,' I said.

He stood up straight, a look of shock on his face. At that moment I couldn't tell if the expression was sincere or if he was acting. He had such an open face, strong features and even white teeth. How could he be anything other than honest?

'Poor Stacey!'

He went to put his arm around me but I shook it off. I backed away and found myself against a wall. He leaned his hand against the bricks and stood close to me. He wasn't touching me but I felt his nearness, I smelled mint on his breath and I felt the heat of his body. So close.

How I had wanted to sink into him, to be a part of him.

'You've misunderstood, Stacey. It was a bit of a laugh. A few mates together, sharing dope and booze . . .'

'And me? Sharing me?'

'No! Nothing as serious as that. It was just relaxed in the bedroom. I thought you wanted . . .'

'I was saying *No*!'

He looked round as if he was afraid someone might hear.

'Girls say no – they don't always mean it. I'm good friends with all the girls that I've spent time with.'

All the girls . . . The words hurt me. Had I thought I was the only one, someone special? I thought of Bella from the Oxfam shop. Maybe there were lots of us.

'What about Melanie? Was she just one of these *girls*?'

I tried to picture this girl that I had never seen. The only image I could get was from behind: long red hair that had never been cut, the ends wispy like that of a baby. I desperately wanted her story to be true, that he had stolen a master's car to go and see her.

'Melanie was different.'

His face had dropped and for the first time he looked away from me as if he couldn't meet my eyes. He had no trouble making eye contact when we were talking about his brother raping me, but now that I had mentioned the girl he loved he baulked.

The black Polo had driven alongside us and was idling, as if waiting to make a quick getaway. I could hear music coming from inside it. Dom was staring out at the road as if he had nothing to do with us.

'That stuff last week,' Harry said, a hint of annoyance in his voice, 'that was just a bit of grown-up play, that's all. No one gets hurt. You didn't get hurt, did you? I looked after you. I spent money on you. I liked you! I still do! Me and my brother and Dom, we usually have a good time, but I can see it confused you. In future it'll just be me and you.'

'No future, no nothing,' I said, pushing him lightly, walking away.

'Stacey!' he called. 'I really like you!'

I kept walking and turned a corner, then I slowed and eventually came to a stop. I took some deep breaths but my heart was thrashing. I put my hand on my chest as if to hold it steady. I looked around and saw that everything was normal – a Friday afternoon after school, the streets full of uniformed school kids ducking and diving their way home, small queues forming outside the fried chicken shop. The pavement felt warm, the slabs cracked across the middle. Scraps of sweet wrappers flew around, avoiding the litter bins. It was Stratford, flaky and grimy in the shadow of the Olympic Park. It wasn't Oxford Street or Kensington, and Harry had come all the way here to see me, to persuade me that I hadn't been raped, I'd just been part of some 'grown-up fun'.

I started to walk again but faltered, my legs feeling shaky. I remembered the phone call I'd overheard the night I'd stayed at the apartment. He'd been talking to his brother and I heard him saying, *Stacey is really sweet. She's nice. I like her.* He did like me. I knew it. I felt it. I wasn't imagining it.

I turned and walked slowly back to the corner.

There was a tiny bit of me that thought, *Why not? Why not see him again? As long as his brother's not around I could spend time with him.* Maybe I hadn't been raped. Possibly I'd made it look as if I was available. They'd misunderstood me. If I started to see Harry now there would be no misunderstanding. He would know that I was just there *for him*.

I peeped round the corner.

The black Polo was still in the same place, but Dom was no longer sitting inside. He had got out and he and Harry were standing on the pavement, leaning back against the car. They were talking to each other. I watched them both. I was trying to work out what expression Harry had. I wanted him to look unhappy, sad, rebuffed. I wanted to see his feelings for me written all over his face. He shrugged though, and I knew that this was the moment I had been written off.

I felt wrung out.

Why had he really come?

Was he just checking up on me? Making sure that I hadn't gone to the police, strengthening the story of his texts; that as far as he was concerned no crime had taken place? I thought about the phone call again between him and his brother. There'd been a disagreement between them and I'd thought it was because his brother hadn't thought me worthy of him. Now, though, something more horrible came into my head. His brother had insisted that *he* had me first. That's why Harry was unresponsive the night before. I'd gone into his room and told him I was no virgin and he had declined. He'd been saving me for his brother.

They stopped talking and Harry looked up in the direction of the school.

A group of girls was walking towards them. They were year nine or ten, no more than that. I watched as Harry called out to them. Dom's face had broken into a smile and he'd stepped away from the car. I saw that he was wearing his beach clothes again, a line of beads around his pale neck. The girls all leaned towards each other and were giggling. One of them squared her shoulders and walked up to Harry in a stately way. She pointed at the car and he turned to it as though he was a salesman. The rest of the girls joined her. I couldn't hear what was being said but I could see that Harry had turned his lights on, as he had that morning for me at Katie's Kitchen. I had been star-struck. The year-ten girls looked the same, all smiley and embarrassed. The regal girl shook her head at something Harry had said and she took a couple of steps away and immediately the others joined her.

I heard his voice above the girls. He was holding his phone in the air and I guessed he was asking for a mobile number. I half expected him to get one of his cards out of his pocket and draw a heart on it and hand it to her.

I didn't want to see that, so I turned and walked towards home. I remembered what Patrice had said to me not thirty minutes before.

If you don't tell someone, if you do nothing, then Harry and his brother can do this again. Do you want some other innocent girl walking into the same thing that you did? You don't want him doing it to someone else, do you?

And I knew that I couldn't just forget the rape. I had to *do* something.

Twenty-Two

The next morning I went to Shoreditch. I headed for my dad's apartment. I knew that Gemma would be out shopping. It was the first time I'd seen him since he'd returned from Corfu and the first time I'd been back in his apartment since the night I'd slept there.

My dad was delighted to see me. He fussed over me, making me a cup of tea and opening a pack of cupcakes. He told me about his holiday in Corfu and the bikes he and Gemma had hired and the boat trip they went on and the fact that Gemma had got seven mosquito bites on one arm. He kept saying, *You should have seen it, Stacey!* and I kept nodding as if I agreed. Then, when I was sitting on the long sofa nibbling the edges of the cake, he suddenly turned serious and asked me the question that I didn't want to answer.

'Stacey, where did you stay on the night you were away from home but you weren't here? Your mum says you won't talk about it. She says you've been really upset since you came back. She's worried about you. I've been concerned.'

My dad was tanned; some of his skin was peeling from one arm. Around his neck he was wearing a strip of leather that held a polished stone. It was disconcerting to see it on him. Since Gemma had come on the scene he'd been wearing jewellery, wristbands and a ring that she'd bought him. He looked odd in it.

'Your mum says you won't talk to her about what it is that's upsetting you.'

I placed my half-eaten cake on the plate.

There was a time when I would have told my dad anything. But I was younger then and the problems I had were things that he could fix. When the kids in school could swim and I couldn't he took me to the local pool every night for a week. He gave me confidence to take off my armbands. When I started to swim on my own, those first tentative strokes, he pointed up at the high diving board and said, *In a couple of weeks we'll have you jumping off that!* If I was having nightmares he would be the one to come and comfort me. If I had no friends to go out with he would take me out somewhere, and Jodie too, if she wanted to come. Even after they split up and my dad lived in various houses, I could get hold of him anytime and confide in him about anything. He never did teach me to jump off the high diving board, although he was willing to do just about anything else that I asked.

Now we had a few minutes to ourselves. The cakes were a nice touch, and without Gemma making polite chit-chat we could talk. It would be good if I could open up to him, but how could I tell him what had happened to me?

How could I?

'It's nothing important,' I said. 'Just girls' stuff.'

Even this didn't usually stop a conversation with my dad. He'd usually say, *I know about periods, Stacey. I'm not an idiot.*

'You mean girls' medical stuff? Or emotional stuff?'

I shrugged.

'You're not pregnant, are you?' he said softly.

'No.' I shook my head. 'No, it's not that.'

And then I thought, *How do I know? I might be pregnant. The condoms I bought were in my bag but weren't used. I could be pregnant. At this very moment I could have a baby growing inside me – a baby that came from a rape.*

'Is it drugs?' my dad said.

I shook my head.

'Is it some boy who's broken your heart?'

I looked at him and felt tears in my eyes. Yes, some boy had broken my heart, but not in the way that he thought. I nodded because he needed an answer and it was the most truthful one I could give him.

'Oh, Stacey . . . We all have to go through these things.'

I heard the key scrape in the door then and knew that Gemma had come back.

'Hello, Stacey,' she said lightly, walking into the room with a carrier bag in each hand.

'Hi,' I said.

'Stacey's a bit down,' my dad said.

'Oh dear.'

Gemma put her bags on the kitchen worktop and turned to look at me.

'What's up, Stacey? Anything we can do to help?'

'I have to go,' I said, standing up. 'I said I'd go round to Patrice's later and I've got essays to work on.'

'Go on, stay for lunch,' she said. 'I've got loads of food.'

151

She was smiling at me. I noticed then that she also had on a leather necklace with a polished stone. She put her fingers on it, just as my dad had done. They were across the room from each other, but I could feel some force pulling them together.

'Thanks, but I better get off.'

My dad gave me a hug at the door.

'You'll find a good lad. Plenty of good ones out there.'

I pulled his front door closed behind me. I stood on the faded West Ham mat and listened as his voice started up again, Gemma's voice coming in, the two of them chattering like best friends.

Along the main road I passed a chemist's and hesitated.

I went inside and looked around. I could see signs for *Skin Products*, *Hair Products*, *Vitamins*. The pharmacy was at the back. I walked along the aisles and after a few minutes I found what I was looking for. I glanced over at the counter. The woman standing behind it was older, maybe in her forties. She had short brown hair and earrings in the shape of pear drops. She was wearing a blue uniform, which was a size too small, the buttons straining across her chest. She made eye contact with me as I walked across and handed her the pregnancy test. She grimaced, a look of sympathy on her face.

'It's for my friend,' I said.

'Course it is, dear.'

She adopted a smile as if to say, *Single teenage mother.* I thought of Jodie. She must have done this very thing when she thought she was pregnant. Had she felt embarrassed or shamed by a shop assistant? But then I remembered that she hadn't done a pregnancy test at all. She missed three periods and only told Mum and Dad and me when it was beginning to show.

The woman tucked the slim packet into a paper bag.

'It *is* for my friend,' I said. 'She's had a scare and I said I'd get it for her.'

I got my cash card out and entered my pin number. She handed me a receipt and her fingers brushed mine.

'Tell your friend not to worry too much. These things work themselves out. It happened to my daughter and now she's got a lovely little boy. We wouldn't be without him.'

'Thanks,' I said.

I left the shop and sighed heavily as the door closed behind me. I walked a few paces and there across the road was the Oxfam shop. I wasn't surprised to see it. I hadn't stumbled upon it by accident. I'd looked up its position on the internet. I knew it was there because I'd intended to visit it and find Bella, the other girl Harry had taken up with.

Twenty-Three

I went into the Oxfam shop. I passed stands of greetings cards and shelves of bric-a-brac. The clothes rails were sorted into colours: white, cream, aquamarine, red, blue. At the back of the shop were the men's clothes and shelves of paperback books and CDs and stacks of records. There was a rack stacked with shoes. In the past I would have rummaged through the clothes and maybe bought a top and a pair of high-heeled shoes or a bag. I might have altered the top or reused the fabric, making something else.

But I had no heart for that now. That morning, before leaving home, I'd looked at all my sewing things and my fashion magazines and bits of fabric and thought, *What's the point?* The prospectus for the London College of Fashion was in my bottom drawer but I hadn't glanced at it since I'd got back from Oxford Street. What had I been thinking? That I would get the right grades in my A levels, go there for three years and end up working for Stella McCartney? It was pathetic. It had always been a pipe dream. I remembered then what Jodie had said to me on the afternoon of my birthday during the row we'd had. *Just because you can sew up a cushion cover doesn't mean you can design clothes for a living.* That day her words had cut me, but now they seemed inconsequential. I'd been hurt much worse since then.

I walked up to the counter. A woman with orange hair was putting sticky labels round bits of jewellery. She was concentrating and had a large paperclip sticking out the side of her mouth.

'Excuse me, do you have a girl called Bella who works here?' She looked up at me. She took the paperclip out.

'We do. She's in the back. Do you want her?'

'Yes, please.'

'Just go and call. She's making teas, I think.'

There was a door at the rear of the shop. It opened onto a brightly lit room with tables and piles of filled black plastic bags, which were lined along one wall. An ironing board had been set up on one side and a woman was using it to press a man's shirt. A couple of elderly women were standing by a table sorting through a box of stuff. There was a radio playing. One of the women looked at me.

'Have you got a donation, dear?'

I shook my head.

'I wanted to see Bella,' I said.

At that moment a girl emerged from a door at the back of the room carrying a tray of hot drinks. She began to sing along with a song that was playing on the radio. Her voice was loud, covering the singer's voice. She stood still, balancing the tray, her eyes partly closed, singing until the end of the song. The women smiled and shook their heads, as if it was something they were used to.

156

'Here we are,' she said when the track had finished.

'Someone to see you, Bella,' one of the women said.

Bella looked up briefly, then back down at the tray. She placed it carefully on the table.

'White tea, two sugars for Marion. White tea, no sugar for Elizabeth and Jessica. And black tea for me and Margaret.'

She handed out the drinks to the women, glancing up at me, then looking back at what she was doing. There were still two mugs left on the tray.

'That's the girl who wants you, Bella,' one of the women said, picking up her mug and blowing the steam from the top of it.

'You want me?' Bella said, picking up one of the remaining drinks. 'I've just got to give this to Jessica.'

I stood back from the door as she passed. She had a quizzical expression on her face. She walked up the shop to the counter and gave the woman there a mug. She mumbled something as she handed it over and the woman answered her. I had a look at her as she was doing it. She was small, like me. She had shoulder-length hair, which was held back by a red stretchy band. She was wearing skinny jeans and a loose black shirt pulled in at the waist with a red elastic belt. She had flat black pumps on her feet.

I could see what Suzie had meant when she said that Bella looked *young*.

She walked back towards me.

'What can I do for you?' she said brightly.

She stood at the door and I backed away a little, keeping space between us. One of the women walked through carrying a tray of glass ornaments.

'Do I know you?' she said when I didn't speak.

'No,' I finally said. 'But we both know the same person. Harry Connaught.'

Her body language changed. Her shoulders dipped and her forehead twitched.

'Harry?' she said.

'Yes. I know you used to see him.'

'So?'

She was guarded. She began to check the fastening on the red belt. When she looked up again her eyes were screwed up, as if she was looking into the sun.

'I wanted to talk to you about him.'

'Did he send you?'

'No . . .'

'Because you can tell him I'm not interested.'

'He didn't.'

'I don't want to see him again. It's over. It has been for weeks.'

'He didn't send me. I'm in the same boat as you. I was seeing him but I'm not any more. That's why I wanted to talk to you . . .'

'I'm not interested.'

With that she walked away into the back room and over to the table where the tray was sitting with the last mug. She had her back to me and started to talk to the woman who was ironing. Her voice had a high fluttery tone to it, as if everything she said flew out of her mouth. She seemed like a happy person. I liked the way her red hairband matched her belt and I admired the flat pumps because it showed that she didn't care that she was small.

I walked into the room. I took the card Harry had given me out of my pocket. I put my hand out to tap her on the shoulder but she spun round before my fingers made contact, as if she knew I would do that.

I held up the card.

'He gave me this. He drew a heart on it. I'm betting he gave you one too.'

The name *Harry Connaught* was just above the heart he had drawn.

Her face fell. She looked up at me with real hurt in her eyes. I took her arm and pulled her towards the door, out of earshot of the women there.

'I'm going over to Costa Coffee. I'll be there for half an hour,' I said. 'I don't really want to talk about Harry at all, but I will if you want. The person I want to talk about is his brother, Marty.'

Her expression hardened. She looked around the room, as if avoiding eye contact. Her mouth seemed to shrink, her lips just thin lines.

'I can't talk about him,' she simply said.

'I'll be there for half an hour. Then I'll go home and you won't see me again. It's up to you if you come.'

I left her standing there and headed out of the shop. I knew then, with certainty, that I hadn't been the first person Marty Connaught had raped.

Twenty-Four

I sat near the window. From where I was I could see the turning further up the high street where I'd gone on the morning I'd first met Harry, where Katie's Kitchen was. I poured my fizzy water into a glass and the bubbles effervesced. I had a strong sensation of that meeting. When he'd talked to me and made me feel important. When he'd given me his card and drawn the heart on it. I'd been ready to pop. Excitement had fizzed in me so that I hadn't gone back to school as I had planned but had made my way to Selfridges, simply because it was a place that he had spoken about.

I'd liked him. I'd *longed* for him, but he'd turned out to be rotten inside.

That morning Harry had said that he'd been staying at a friend's place overnight. I wondered if that was how he had met Bella, wandering around Shoreditch, perhaps bumping into her as she came out of the shop. Or maybe she used Katie's Kitchen for her lunch and he'd sat at the same table.

The door opened and I watched as Bella came in. She had a bag over her shoulder that had fringes hanging from it. I couldn't help but like the way she looked, her style. The red elastic belt was vintage, I was sure, and as she got closer I could see that the bag was suede. In the past I might have drawn her outfit in my sketchbook. She hooked the bag over the back of the chair opposite me and sat down. One of the baristas gave her a questioning look but she didn't seem to notice.

'How did you know about me?' she said, getting straight to the point.

'Dom's girlfriend, Suzie, told me that Harry had a *type* of girl. She mentioned your name. She said he had been seeing you before he met me. She told me where you worked.'

'So, what was the *type*?'

'Young. We both looked *young*.'

'How old are you?'

'Seventeen. I'm in the lower sixth. You?'

'Sixteen. Doing my GCSEs.'

Bella was only sixteen. Younger than me.

'What happened to you? With Harry, I mean,' she said. 'Do you mind telling me?'

'Not at all.'

I told her everything. I explained how I'd met Harry and what we'd done over the two days: the taxi rides, the drinks, staying in the apartment, the Whistles dress. I explained about him introducing me to the Selfridges buyer and how I liked to design clothes and how I wanted to go to the London College of Fashion. I found myself explaining more than I thought I would about my plans for the future. I didn't want her to see me as some dopey teenager who had been a pushover.

She shook her head slowly.

'It's weird that Harry introduced you to the buyer at Selfridges, because I sing,' she said. 'I mean, I'm a *singer*. I'm in a choir and I go for lessons. I told Harry about it and he said his brother knew a record producer and he would introduce me so that I could find out about the music industry.'

I looked at her in dismay. We'd both been taken in by his supposed generosity.

'How stupid I was,' she said.

'Not just you,' I said. 'Me too. Maybe not even *just* us.'

I finished my story then, telling her about being raped by Marty Connaught. I didn't go into details, didn't say that I was already there on the bed, wanting to be with Harry. I just said that he'd come into the bedroom and forced me to have sex. I didn't even say that Harry had been *in there* at the same time. I was too ashamed. She was listening intently, her eyes clinging to my face. Her skin was reddening, as if she was ready to burst into tears. As I spoke her hand moved across the table and grabbed mine. Tears bubbled up in her eyes. I let go of her hand so that she could wipe them away. I didn't know whether she was crying for me or herself.

'Let me get you a tea,' I said.

I went to the counter and bought two black teas. I was feeling odd. I was upset, but at the same time I was feeling lighter. It was the first time that I'd explained what had happened to someone who really seemed to understand. This was sad in itself. It was bad enough that I had gone through it, but I was sure that she had too. That's why my story had upset her. As I paid for the teas I looked round to see her blowing her nose and wiping her eyes.

163

'Your friend all right?' the barista said.

'She'll be OK.'

When I returned she told me about her relationship with Harry.

'He came into the shop and I served him. He bought a couple of books. I said to him, *Why's a posh bloke like you buying books from a charity shop?* He said that he'd come into the shop just to talk to me. He said he'd been building up courage for at least an hour. He asked me if I'd meet him after work to go for a drink. And I did. That's how it started. We spent time together over the next couple of weeks. I went over to Kensington and met him after school and some days he came over here. I thought it was romantic, like Romeo and Juliet. He was rich, I was poor, and yet we wanted to be together. We went out a few times at night and he stayed over at a friend's place nearby. We saw Dominic and Suzie a couple of times.'

I drank my tea. She fiddled with her hairband, pushing it further back on her head so that some strands of hair escaped.

'There was a weekend when his parents went out and he asked me to go over to his house for the day. I got there about ten on Saturday morning. His brother was there. Well, he was around. He took the dog out and then he made some lunch and asked us to share it. He was chatty. He asked me about my plans for a singing career. I told him I was going to uni to get my degree so that I had a career to fall back on in case the singing didn't work. He said I should be more ambitious and not think about things not working out. He said he'd arrange a meeting with a guy he knew who was a junior music producer. He was really nice.'

I tried to picture Marty Connaught but the image was vague. I remembered his face and his big stomach, but I couldn't really see him clearly. I avoided trying to recall what he'd looked like in the bedroom of the apartment.

'Harry and I went up to his room. Then Harry got a call and he said he had to pop out. There was some problem with Dominic and his dad, some row. He said he'd be an hour at the most. He told me to watch television or listen to music, to make myself at home.'

Bella took the hairband off and her hair fell forward. It covered the sides of her face.

'He was gone about ten minutes, maybe a bit more, when Marty came into Harry's room. He sat on the end of the bed. He said he'd just spoken to the guy, the music producer, on the phone and he was keen to see me. I was excited. I said, *Thank you*. He said, *What about a thank-you kiss?* I felt a bit silly but I moved over and went to kiss him on the cheek, only he turned his face so the kiss was on the mouth and then . . .'

Bella pulled her bag from the back of her seat and rummaged around in it. She took out a hair tie and she gathered up her hair and put it on.

'There's not much more to tell. He pushed me down on the bed and lay on top of me. I was wearing a skirt so I didn't have much of a chance. If I'd had my jeans on . . .'

She looked away, her fingers playing with the hairband.

'When was this?'

'Eight weeks ago today.'

'And you didn't go to the police.'

She shook her head. Her mouth had gone tight as if there was more to say.

'Why not?'

It was a funny question for me to ask considering that I hadn't gone to the police either.

'I told Harry when he came back and he . . . he seemed to *blame* me. He said that I had given his brother the wrong signals. That it was my fault. I expected him to be comforting me but instead it seemed that I was trying to make excuses to him. In the end he said he *forgave* me. I left his house that day feeling that I'd done something wrong. Then I texted him and said I didn't want to see him again.'

'But you still didn't go to the police?'

She shook her head.

'I understand. Neither did I. This is one of the reasons I wanted to talk to you. I didn't go because the circumstances of my rape made me think that no one would believe me or that it was partly my fault that it had happened. If you and I *both* went to the police, there could be no doubt about Marty Connaught's guilt.'

She was still shaking her head.

'Why not?'

'Because . . .' She shrugged.

'What?'

'Because I started to see Harry again. He came to the shop and I guess I was just smitten. He talked me round. He said it had all been a misunderstanding and that we shouldn't let it affect our relationship. So I kept seeing him. I had sex with him, three times. The last time his brother turned up.'

'He didn't . . . Not again . . .'

'No, no. I got out. I just ran and left the house. I knew then that I'd made a fool of myself and I haven't seen him since.'

'Oh, Bella . . .'

'Even after his brother raped me I stayed with him. What would the police say about that? I just have to accept that I made a stupid mistake and forget it.'

I made a stupid mistake and forget it.

Hadn't I been thinking the very same thing? Hadn't I tried to persuade myself of just that approach? *If I could view it as some kind of accident . . . it would hurt for a while but it would fade.* She sounded just like me.

'But can you?'

'Why not? It's raw now. I think about it a lot, but over time I will forget. This time next year it will just be a distant memory.'

We left the coffee shop soon after. We swapped mobile numbers. She made me promise that if I went to the police I wouldn't bring her into it. I did promise. I walked her to the charity shop and she gave me a hug. It felt like we were old friends. Although we'd only just met, we had more in common than most people.

I walked away and wondered if I'd ever see her again.

Twenty-Five

Patrice and I were lying on the trampoline. The garden was black around us. The lights of the kitchen seemed far away and it was if we were on a boat anchored in a bay, looking back at a town on the shore. I had a large cushion under my head and she was sharing a corner of it, lying at a right angle. I could feel her hair tickling my face. We were both a bit drunk. We'd had a bottle of freezing-cold white wine with some noodles and egg fried rice that Patrice's mum had made for us.

Earlier in the evening Patrice had treated my hair. She'd put a special conditioner on it, then blown it dry so that it was straight and glossy. I told her she should be a hairdresser, not a barrister, when she grew up, but she told me not to be so stupid.

We'd watched a movie that she'd downloaded and then we'd gone on Facebook and saw what was happening. She'd pointed out a flyer that Benji Ashe had uploaded about a session of DJing he was doing for an end-of-term party for year-ten students. I was surprised. Patrice had given me a look. *What do you think he buys all those vinyls for?* she'd said. I hadn't thought about it at all. In the weeks I'd gone out with him I'd hardly asked him about himself. I simply hadn't been interested. Now, lying back on the trampoline, I thought about how badly I'd treated him.

'You know that thing you don't want to talk about?' Patrice said, her voice soft.

When I'd first arrived at her house earlier I'd asked Patrice if we could just ignore that subject for one night and she'd agreed. She'd managed to keep her promise all evening, but I'd noticed from time to time how she'd been on the brink of saying something, how she'd started with, *Stacey? . . . Oh nothing*. I knew for the last hour or so that she'd been bursting with it.

'Yes,' I said.

'Can I just say a couple of things?'

'OK. Then we don't talk about it again.'

'Sure.'

The sky was flat and dense and there were no stars or moon that I could see. There was one light twinkling, moving about. I thought it was probably a helicopter but I couldn't hear it. They were probably looking down at huge swathes of black cut up by the lights of cars and street lighting. I remembered seeing just that when I was in a plane that was circling around, coming back from a holiday abroad when my mum and dad were still together. I'd had the window seat, even though Jodie had wanted it.

Patrice had sat up and the trampoline sank to one side with her weight. I pushed myself and my pillow to the opposite side to balance it.

'Have you made plans for a pregnancy test?'

'I've bought the kit. I have to wait until fourteen days after unprotected sex, then I use it.'

'What about STDs?'

Sexually transmitted diseases. I'd thought about it and even looked up the phone number of my GP but couldn't bring myself to make an appointment.

'I haven't done anything about that yet.'

'They'll help you with all this at the Rape Crisis Centre. They do it all. I've been reading up on it. Here's the other thing,' she went on, her voice accelerating in case I told her to stop. 'You can go there, tell them everything and still decide not to go to the police. You can show them your story – even though it's not finished. There's no pressure on you and it's completely confidential.'

Patrice was close enough that I could see her face, even though it was dark. She looked very earnest. I felt bad. I hadn't been straight with her. My story was finished but in limbo on my laptop. I hadn't told her about Harry coming up to the school on Friday afternoon, or about my visit to the charity shop to meet Bella earlier that day. I'd kept these things back for a whole variety of reasons. Mostly because I was so unclear about what I wanted to do and I knew that Patrice was strong-willed enough to put pressure on me. Especially if she knew the truth about how Harry had been texting me and how he had continued to see Bella after his brother had raped her. The word *grooming* came into my mind. Patrice was my best friend, but I couldn't be swayed by her. This was a decision I had to make by myself.

'What about . . . ?' I said, after a minute. 'What if I wait until the end of next week? I'll take the pregnancy test and I should have finished my story by then. Then you can read it and I'll decide what to do.'

171

'OK,' she said.

She gave a sort of hopeless smile, as if she knew already what I'd decided.

'Let's not talk about it any more tonight,' I said, grabbing the sleeve of her jumper and holding onto it.

'I'll go and see if there's any more wine,' she said.

When I left her house just after lunch the next day she was getting ready to go to Shelly's. She was helping her with an essay on Law and Morals. She gave me a hug and told me to *keep strong*. I walked home feeling good. I had no bad feelings at all about her seeing Shelly. I knew from the things she'd said and the way she'd looked after me over the last week that our friendship was solid.

I was also feeling calm about my own situation. The things I had said to Patrice, about waiting till the following Friday to do the pregnancy test and then deciding what to do, had made me feel much better. I had five days to think about it. Five days in which to decide which way my life was going to go.

I got back to my street at about two thirty. I could feel a spring in my step. I'd told Jodie I would look after Tyler that afternoon because she was going round to see one of her old friends. I had some work to do for school, but I could do that after Tyler went to bed.

I honestly felt as though a weight had fallen from my shoulders.

I went into my house determined to smile at Mum and Jodie and not show my usual miserable face.

But when I walked in Jodie came rushing out of the kitchen.

'You've got a visitor!' she said.

'Who?' I said.

My first thought was that it was Benji Ashe. Perhaps he had found something else of mine around his house and was using it as an excuse to see me.

'It's your boyfriend's brother.'

'Boyfriend?'

'Yeah – you kept that to yourself! Sounds posh as well.'

I walked into the kitchen. My mum was sitting at the table drinking tea from a cup and saucer. In the seat opposite her was Marty Connaught.

'Hello, Stacey,' he said.

Twenty-Six

I was stunned. I didn't say anything and could feel my mum's eyes on me. I looked round for Tyler but he wasn't there. I was glad of that. After the shock of seeing Marty Connaught there, in my house, talking to my family, the one thing I couldn't bear was the idea of Tyler being in his presence.

'Sit down, Stacey. I've just made this tea,' my mum said.

'I don't want it,' I said.

I hadn't moved. I was standing at the door of the room. Jodie had edged around me and was in the kitchen, leaning back against the fridge. She had a look of delight on her face, as if she'd caught me doing something I shouldn't.

'Stacey didn't tell us about her boyfriend,' my mum said, directing her comment to Marty Connaught. 'But she has been acting a bit strange lately. Now we know the reason.'

'Why are you here?' I said, cutting across her.

'Stacey!'

I ignored my mum and stared at him. He had on a dark suit with a red tie. He looked smart, as if he was on his way to a wedding. I focused on his face and felt my throat tighten. My ribs seemed to contract so that I was just sipping in air. He was there *in my house*. He was smiling widely, like a cheery uncle visiting. I glared at him.

'Stacey, where's your manners?' my mum said, looking awkward, placing her hands on the side of the teapot as if to check that it was still warm.

'No problem, Mrs Woods,' Marty Connaught said. 'I was just passing. We have family friends who live in Shoreditch and as I was over this way Harry asked me to drop this by.'

'How come we haven't met this *Harry*?' Jodie said.

I ignored her as he pointed to a package on the table. It had been gift-wrapped and there was ribbon around it.

'A present for you, Stacey. That's a nice surprise,' my mum said.

'You should go, now,' I said briskly, pulling the door open behind me.

'Honestly, you're being so rude,' my mum said, looking put out, embarrassed. 'I'm so sorry,' she said, turning to Marty Connaught. 'Stacey's been a bit under the weather lately.'

'Don't apologise for me, Mum. He's going.'

Marty Connaught stood up and fiddled with the knot of his tie. His jacket fell open and I could see his stomach protruding, the buttons on his shirt not quite doing up. I felt sick at the sight of him, a memory flashing in my head of him lying on top of me, his weight pinning me down, his hand pushing my legs apart. For a second I felt faint and leaned against the work surface to steady myself. I tried to block out the image of him, then turned and walked out into the hall towards the front door. I could feel my hands and arms trembling. From upstairs I could hear Tyler whimpering, like he did when he was waking up from a nap.

'Jodie, Tyler's awake,' I said firmly.

I opened the front door and held it wide so that there was no mistaking the fact that I wanted Marty Connaught to leave. Jodie came out of the kitchen and headed upstairs, turning for a moment and whispering loudly, *What's going on?*

I could hear my mum's voice, apologetic, and the answers he gave – gracious, polite, conciliatory. *Don't worry! I shouldn't have come unannounced. Maybe Stacey and my brother have had a falling-out. You know what young people are like!*

He came out into the hall. He barely glanced at me, his face stony.

'Goodbye, Mrs Woods,' he called, and walked past me.

I followed him out and pulled the front door shut behind me.

'How dare you come to my house,' I said, outraged.

'Calm down, Stacey, calm down.'

'Don't come near me or my family!'

'Just trying to be friendly, that's all,' he said, pulling his mobile phone out of his jacket pocket. 'Harry said he saw you the other day. He said you seemed a bit upset. I just wanted to make sure you were all right. That's why I came.'

All the time he spoke he was tapping at his mobile phone. Then he put it away.

'Just go away,' I said.

'I will. When I'm sure you're not in a mix-up about what happened last week. I think you were confused, that's all. I just wanted to make sure we were all on the same page.'

'*The same page!*'

I was astounded. I couldn't believe the words he was using, what he was trying to do. It was as if he was talking about a work matter, some subject that had been discussed at a meeting, not the rape of a girl.

'Stacey.'

He shook his head in a disappointed way. He took a step towards me, reached out and touched my hand with his fingers. I pulled my hand away.

'What happened last week was a bit of fun. Things went too far *for you*, but don't say anyone forced you. You need to be clear about that. Because if you tried to say that they had, my family would make life very unpleasant for you.'

'You're threatening me?'

'Don't misunderstand me. Not at all. No one would hurt you, course not. We're civilised people, Stacey. What I mean is that we would make things uncomfortable for you. After all,' he lowered his voice, 'you weren't a virgin, were you? You were already undressed. And am I right in thinking your sister had a baby when she was fourteen? These things won't look good in a court of law, Stacey. Trust me, I know.'

I couldn't speak.

'I'll just wait for my cab in the street,' he said. 'Oh, don't forget your present. Harry really did buy it. He likes you. You should call him.'

He walked out of my front garden and onto the pavement. Just then a black cab came along the street and pulled up sharply. He got in without a look back. I watched it drive away, my emotions shrivelling, my nerve shrinking, my heart drained.

I went inside in a daze. My sister was standing at the bottom of the stairs holding Tyler, who had just woken up. His face was puce and he had one knuckle at his mouth.

'You kept that a secret!' Jodie said.

I walked past her, straight into the kitchen where my mum was clearing away the teapot and cups.

'What's up, Stacey? I gather by the way you reacted that you don't like that man. Is it true about his brother?'

'I can't explain, Mum. I just can't. Not right this minute.'

I picked up the gift-wrapped parcel and pulled off the ribbon. Then I tore at the paper. I could feel that it was a book of some sort, and when I'd unwrapped it I didn't know what to say. It was a beautiful hardback: the V&A's *One Hundred Years of Fashion Photography*. I looked at the price – thirty pounds. I let it fall open and saw glossy pictures of fashions over the years.

It was thoughtful. It was exactly the right present for me. Patrice had bought me a book about fashion for my birthday and I had been thrilled with it. But that book had been bought with love. This one had been bought with some other intention. To sweeten me up? To make me believe that I hadn't been used by Harry and his brother? To persuade me that it really hadn't been rape, just a misunderstanding, and that we could all go on as if nothing had actually happened.

'It's a very lovely gift,' my mum said tentatively. 'Seeing as you're so interested in fashion.'

I shook my head,

'No, Mum. It's not a gift. It's a bribe.'

I took the book out of the back door, took the lid off our dustbin and dropped it in. Jodie was standing watching me.

'Something's really wrong, isn't it?' she said as I passed her by.

I nodded. She put her hand on my arm, her fingers grabbing my flesh. Her forehead was wrinkled up.

'Is there anything I can do to help?'

Her face seemed suddenly younger, her scowl gone, her eyes crinkly and hopeful, as if she was my little sister again, creeping into my bedroom and asking me if she could tidy up my felt-tip pens.

'No, I have to help myself now,' I said.

Twenty-Seven

I didn't wait until Friday to make my decision. The next morning, instead of going to school, I sat on my bed and decided to make a list of the good and bad things in my life. I had a notepad and a pen in my hand and I was about to divide the page in half, but I thought, *Why? Why bother?* There was really only one bad thing in my life. I didn't need to see a written list to know what it was.

The word *rape* didn't seem to cover it though. It seemed too slight, too simple to describe what had happened. I thought of other words: assault, betrayal, robbery. Because I *had* been physically assaulted; there were no scars but nonetheless my body had been abused. I *had* suffered a betrayal by someone I cared about. I *had* been robbed of my faith in people.

I opened up my laptop and found the website of the Rape Crisis Centre. With trembling fingers I rang the number on the screen. All the while I was looking round my room at familiar things: the chest of drawers, the wardrobe, the storage unit full of my sewing bits and pieces. Above it was the row of hooks on which scarves and swathes of fabric hung. There was my big armchair in the bay of the window and the table beside it. From downstairs I could hear Jodie and Tyler.

As the number rang I felt myself tensing up and thought about cutting the call. There was still time to pull back, to close up the laptop and keep my secrets to myself. I didn't though. The ringtone sounded loudly in my ear and then, finally, a woman answered the call.

'Hello? Rape Crisis. May I help you?'

'I . . .'

I stopped, my eyes filling with tears. The woman sounded nice, sympathetic. What would she think of me when she heard my story? Would she be understanding? Or would she think that I had brought it on myself?

'I . . .'

'Take your time, my dear.'

Her voice was soft and slow.

'Let me tell you a bit about who we are. Rape Crisis is a support agency for people who have suffered a serious assault. We are completely confidential and want to help. We will put no pressure on you to bring a case and we will offer you all the support we can.'

'I . . .'

The words just wouldn't come out. I felt like I was high up somewhere and the world was a long way below. I remembered then the diving board at the swimming pool. After I learned to swim my dad was going to show me how to jump off it, but he never had.

The voice on the other end of the line continued.

'I will hold this line for as long as it takes. I'm in no rush for you to speak. I'll listen to your silence because I know you are going through a decision-making process. When you've decided

182

I will be here to listen to you and help you to do what it is you want to do. I can be your friend here. You are not alone. That's what we want you to know.'

'I . . .'

I started to cry. She must have been able to hear me. I was tottering, at the edge of the board. The pool was miles below. I just had to take a step and jump into the silky blue water. I could hear her continuing to talk calmly, her words measured. Her voice was liquid, her words merging one into the other. Then she stopped. The line was silent, like deep water. I just had to find the courage to dive in. I counted to five in my head and took a leap.

'My name is Stacey Woods and I was raped,' I said.

Anne Cassidy

Anne Cassidy was born in London in 1952. She was an awkward teenager who spent the Swinging Sixties stuck in a convent school trying, dismally, to learn Latin. She was always falling in love and having her heart broken. She worked in a bank for five years until she finally grew up. She then went to college before becoming a teacher for many years. In 2000 Anne became a full time writer, specialising in crime stories and thrillers for teenagers. In 2004 LOOKING FOR JJ was published to great acclaim, going on to be shortlisted for the 2004 Whitbread Prize and the 2005 Carnegie Medal. Follow Anne at www.annecassidy.com or on Twitter: @annecassidy6

HOT KEY BOOKS

Thank you for choosing a Hot Key book.

If you want to know more about our authors
and what we publish, you can find us online.

You can start at our website

www.hotkeybooks.com

And you can also find us on:

We hope to see you soon!